ISLE
OF
OSTIN

The Ostin Heir

Copyright ©2022 Michelle Dare

Cover Design: Michelle Dare

Photography: Eric McKinney, 6:12 Photography

Model: Dave W.

Editing: Barren Acres Editing

Proofreading: Joanne Thompson

This is a work of fiction. Any resemblance to actual persons, living or dead, business establishments, events, or locales is entirely coincidental.

All rights reserved. No part of this book may be reproduced or transmitted in any form or by any means without express written permission from the author/publisher.

No Generative AI Training Use. The Author expressly prohibits using the Work in any manner for purposes of training artificial intelligence technologies to generate text, including without limitation, technologies that are capable of generating works in the same style or genre as the Work. The Author reserves all rights to license uses of the Work for generative AI training and development of machine learning language models.

Author's Note: No artificial intelligence (A.I.) or predictive language software was used in any part of the creation of this book.

FOLLOW MICHELLE DARE

Michelle's Ream
Michelle's Reader Group
Michelle's Newsletter
Michelle's Website
Michelle's Amazon
Michelle's Facebook
Michelle's TikTok
Michelle's Instagram
Michelle's Pinterest
Michelle's BookBub

THE OSTIN HEIR

Seventy years ago, Theo Ostin witnessed his family murdering a town of humans. He also watched as stakes were driven into his parents' chests. Since then, he's lived on an island no one knows still exists, let alone that he survived.

He prefers it that way.

There's something about Desolate Beach that calls to Paxton Huxley on a visceral level. He doesn't understand why, but he gives in and stands on the sand every chance he gets.

One day, a man gives him a note and a pendant before vanishing right in front of his eyes. The catch? Paxton now works for a royal vampire.

But is it really a job when he starts to desire the man he's helping?

Maybe, just maybe, amid the hell they're both in, they'll find something more important. Something they will fight to the death to keep. Love.

CONTENT WARNING

Please note that this book contains the following: descriptive violence including death, drinking of blood by humans and vampires, assault, anxiety, off-page rape, and off-page suicide. If any of these are triggers for you, please proceed with caution.

PROLOGUE
THEO

Seventy Years Ago

It didn't used to be this way. My family's thirst was under control. They'd never targeted humans before. But something changed tonight. They became different. Insatiable. Nothing else mattered but drinking, killing, destroying.

They fled our home and went into the streets. Left under the cloak of darkness, no moon in the sky to illuminate their way.

Not sure what was going on, I got up from my bed and pushed the heavy drapes aside to peer out the window.

My parents, aunts, uncles, and cousins were murdering an entire town in a blood frenzy. I left my room, went down the stairs, and out the door, trying to understand what was happening. I watched helplessly as they tore out throats, drank until they drained the humans dry.

The town was small, nothing but adult humans who enjoyed living amongst a large family of vampires. Humans we dined with. Ones we laughed with. People who lived side by side with us. Knew who we were and weren't afraid.

I begged my family to stop. At only ten years old, I didn't

have the strength they did. No matter how hard I tugged on my mother's arm, she wouldn't release the man she had in her clutches. Her fangs dug into his neck as blood trickled down his pale skin, life slowly leaving him.

Mother turned toward me with a hiss, her lips coated in crimson. I thought she was going to lunge for me. I was wrong. It wasn't me she was after. I was her child. Somewhere in her mind, she must have recognized that. It wasn't enough to stop her from taking others' lives though.

I hid. Couldn't take anymore. There were bodies everywhere, skin gray in color. They were people I liked who were dead. I tucked myself behind the corner of a building and hoped no one saw me. I tried to block out the sounds, the smells. But Leven found me. He pulled me into his arms and tried to run. As much as I didn't want to see what was going on, I didn't want to leave my family either. They were all I knew. I screamed, told him to put me down. He wouldn't relent.

Leven was only a few steps away when a loud cry of anger came from the surrounding streets. Humans poured from alleyways. They were holding weapons. Not the kind used in war. I knew what they looked like. These were wooden stakes made from maple trees that had been struck by lightning. Instead of burning, they turned midnight black and hardened. The stakes had pointed ends, made with one goal in mind: to kill those I loved.

I froze in Leven's arms; my voice seized in my throat. They didn't care about Leven and me. They were focused on my family, the ones covered in the blood of their victims. As the humans rushed past us, they blazed a trail of fire on the ground. The scent of gasoline burned my nose. The fire heated my skin, had me twisting away from it.

We were moving again. Leven dragged me as I tried to

wiggle free to run back. I might have been young, but I knew how to fight. "No!" I cried, reaching for my parents.

Leven didn't stop. He kept going.

The last thing I saw before we rounded a corner out of sight were the stakes being plunged into my parents' chests. They were focused on quenching their thirsts, not listening to the sounds around them.

Something happened to cause my family to do this. They were happy before. They coexisted with the humans. Never seeking them out like this. Tonight, they weren't the family I knew. They were something from a nightmare.

Could it happen to me too? Could I become like them?

With tears running down my cheeks, Leven dragged me to the beach, to the water's edge, and placed me in a boat. I tried to get free again, but darkness overtook my vision and I succumbed to the abyss of nothing.

1

PAXTON

Present Day

Desolate Beach. It wasn't always called that. I didn't remember what its name was before the night vampires ravaged the beach town in Delaware. Luckily, the neighboring town heard what was happening and came to kill the vampires before they could hurt more.

The ground was scorched. Fire burned everything down except the stone structures. They were nothing but shells of the buildings left. Even the beach had granules of black sand mixed into the normal tan colored ones. The black drifted into the sea like inky fingers reaching out for help.

My feet sank into the sea-drenched sand as I looked out into the Atlantic. Desolate was farther down the Delaware coast, closer to the Maryland border. A low-lying layer of fog permanently hung around. Prevented me from seeing too much. Nothing like the beaches north of here. They were sunny this time of year, warm, filled with vacationers looking to get away.

Yet, I came here. I always did.

Something drew me to Desolate. It was nothing I could explain. I had theories though.

Maybe it was that the beach recognized another lost soul in me.

Maybe it was my curiosity about what happened here all those years ago. Stories had been passed down from the men who were there, who killed the vampires.

Or maybe it was just my shit luck in life. No friends. No family.

Whatever the case was, I found solace in Desolate, looking out at the fog rolling over the ocean. Inhaling the salty air deep into my lungs like it could breathe new life into me.

I'd never been anywhere else. Lived in this state my whole life. Bounced around from foster home to foster home until I aged out. No one wanted to permanently claim me, to make me part of their family. But that was okay. I learned early on not to depend on anyone but myself.

My feet took me north as I carried my flip-flops in hand. I looked back at the town, at the charred remains that were never demolished. Never taken away to make room for new buildings. No, they were kept here as a reminder to the other vampires in the country. That if they attempted what was done in Desolate, they'd feel the same pain. They'd get staked, killed, an end brought to their long lives.

When I crossed from the limits of Desolate, I stepped onto a sunny beach with gulls flying overhead and the sound of people enjoying themselves filtered to me. We called this one Sparkling Beach because of the way the sand always glistened like diamonds when the sun hit it. Instead of heading toward the happy people, I walked onto the long pier. Boats could dock at the end. Not big ones, the water wasn't deep enough for that, but the smaller ones.

At the end, I leaned against the railing and took in the stark contrast between where I stood and Desolate. It was like there was an invisible line dividing the two. One was light, full of joy. The other was gray, full of dread. Which was odd considering I never felt that when I was there.

A noise from my left caught my attention. The sound of the water lapping against a boat. Looking down, I saw a man on the small vessel. It was a nicer one with beautiful red wood that shined like it was well taken care of. Bags of groceries and other things filled it, which he was securing.

It made me wonder where he was going with them. I glanced out at sea and didn't notice any bigger ships there he could be taking the supplies to.

Shoes hitting the gangway drew my gaze over again. The man was walking up. I stepped out of the way to make room for him but didn't leave the end of the pier. I wanted to stay here a little while longer. It wasn't like I had anywhere to be. I wasn't scheduled to work.

"Hello," he said when he stood on the pier near me. He wore tan cargo shorts and a white polo shirt was tucked into them. He had on sneakers that looked worn but well loved. Light blond hair was mussed from the ocean breeze. And he stood several inches shorter than my six-foot, two-inch frame.

"Hi," I replied. I wasn't shy but also wasn't someone who wanted any attention on me.

He came to stand beside me, looking out at the ocean. "It doesn't get old, does it?"

"What's that?"

"The juxtaposition of the two beaches."

"Most people around here prefer not to look at it. They like to pretend it doesn't exist."

"Yet, there it is." He turned toward me, resting his elbow on the salt battered wood railing. "You don't seem to mind it."

I looked at the fog, the way sun didn't shine brightly there.

"There's something... interesting about it." I didn't want to say beautiful, even if I thought it at times. What happened there was horrific and tragic. But when I strictly looked at the sand, the waves, the empty buildings, it had a beautiful, haunting aspect to it.

"I think so too," he said, drawing my attention back to him. The man was probably in his mid-fifties, if I had to guess. Had some wrinkles by his eyes and around his mouth. Nothing prominent. I wouldn't have noticed if he was farther away. "Have you ever seen one?"

It took me a moment to realize what he was asking me, but I still wanted to confirm I was right. "A vampire?"

He nodded.

"No. There haven't been any spotted on the coast from Maine to South Carolina. There are rumored to be some in Georgia and Florida, but none from the major families."

In high school, we were taught about vampires. How there were four families who were prominent in the United States and considered themselves royals. There was no one king over all vampires. They each had their own within their family. Someone who ruled them, kept them in line, dealt with any politics with the humans, and so on. There were vampires around the world as well, some royals, others not.

The fifth family, the one who resided here, was wiped out. They called the town now known as Desolate Beach home. None of them remained.

There were other vampires, of course, who lived amongst humans. Ones who were lesser than the others, not part of the royal families. Less money. Less notoriety. Less everything. They didn't bother anyone, knowing they could easily be killed.

Once the humans knew how to take out an entire family, they spread the word. People armed themselves. Sought out the lightning trees as I called them. Made stakes. Always prepared should anything like that happen again. It hadn't, thankfully.

Then there were the fanatics. Humans who wanted to be drank from. Who stood at the gates of the royals' massive homes and begged to be let in. The vampires signed a peace agreement with the United States government and the others around the world where they were located. They agreed they wouldn't drink from humans, unless they asked to be changed and brought into their family. And in return, they were left alone to live their lives. Humans and vampires coexisting.

"Rumors," the man hummed, reminding me we were talking before I let my thoughts carry me away.

"Yes."

"Some could be in hiding."

"It's possible."

He hummed again and glanced back out at the ocean. The Desolate side had calm waves, though I had seen them churn up from time to time, getting wilder, angry if that were possible.

The man reached over and placed his hand on top of mine. Something happened. An icy cold spread through me. I gasped and pulled away, putting a few feet between us.

"What did you do?" I asked. I'd never felt anything like that before.

"You're alone, correct? No one claims you as theirs? No girl-friend or boyfriend?"

"That's none of your business," I said in a hard tone, while clutching the hand he touched to my chest. The ice in my veins receding slowly.

"Ah, but it is, Paxton Huxley. I have something for you." He reached into his pocket and pulled out at least six different colored pieces of paper. He flipped through them until he found the one he was looking for, then pocketed the others. "Take this." He extended his arm and opened his hand. In his palm sat a pastel pink note with something scrawled on it I couldn't read and a wooden pendant on a leather cord.

"I'm not taking anything from you. Not after whatever you did to me."

"I had to make sure you were the one."

"The one what?"

"The one to take my place."

"Listen, I'm not sure what you're getting at, but I have a job. I work sixty hours a week at minimum wage with no overtime pay. I don't need to add more to it." And the company I worked for didn't give a shit what the government said about paying overtime. They did what they wanted and didn't face consequences for it.

The man shook his head. "This isn't a *job*. It's what you've been waiting for. A purpose. Something to fill the void in your chest."

How did he know that? All my life I felt like I was searching for something. When I was younger, I thought it was a family to love me. As a teenager, it was my birth parents. But that road ended fast when I found out they'd both died of drug overdoses. Now, I felt lost. Didn't think I belonged anywhere but didn't have the money to travel and find where I fit. Every dollar I earned went toward bills or food. Insurance on my piece of shit car.

I started walking backward down the pier, keeping the man in front of me. "No," I told him.

He watched me go and just as I was about to turn around and run, he grabbed his chest. His knees buckled. He landed hard on the wooden decking. I looked around, no one was here. There were people on the beach, but this far out on the pier, no one would hear me or care.

"Shit," I muttered and rushed toward the man. He was

creepy but I couldn't let him die here. I crouched down at his side and dug my phone out of my pocket.

His hand gripped mine holding the phone. "You can't save me," he rasped. "Take these." He pried open my fingers, so my phone dropped to the pier with a thud and placed the note and pendant in my hand. The moment the warm wood of the pendant touched my bare skin, a light shined from it in a brilliant sapphire color.

Looking over at the man, I had to blink a few times to make sure what I was seeing was real. The man was fading in front of me. Going from flesh and bone to something like a ghost before he disappeared altogether.

I gasped and fell back on my ass, shuffling away from him. What just happened?

My palms hit the wood so I could push myself up. Something crinkled in my hand. When I stood, I remembered he handed me a piece of paper. That note in my palm was crumpled now but I could still read it.

Never surrender what I gave you. Get in the boat. It will know where to go. Don't hesitate. A life depends on you bringing the contents within home.

This was madness. I shook my head, yet my hand clutched the pendant and note tightly. I walked over to the edge where the gangway was and peered down at the boat. Nothing was different about it. Still filled with bags and a few boxes.

I looked toward the beach where there were happy families playing with their kids. Sandcastles were being built. People were laughing. Some splashing in the water. That wasn't my reality. I never had fun like that. Never had anyone care enough to take me to the beach when I was younger.

Then I glanced over my shoulder toward Desolate. The place that called to me. Where I felt more like myself.

Was I really considering this? Taking a boat from a man who vanished before my eyes?

There was nothing waiting for me at my studio apartment besides humidity, thanks to no air-conditioning, and a lumpy bed that hurt my back more than anything. Oh, and a job I hated cleaning office buildings at night once everyone went home.

Fuck it. I had nothing to lose. At least this way I'd know what happened when I got in the boat.

2

THEO

Leven should have been back by now. He left to do the bi-weekly stock-up for food and other necessities. Something he'd done countless times over the years. Today, it was taking longer than normal.

I paced within the castle walls, looking out onto the ocean which was dark and foreboding. It always looked that way around the island. Leven said the farther away he got, the brighter it became, which made sense since it was me who cast the area in the thick fog that hung around. I hadn't felt the sun on my face in seventy years. Hadn't left the island either since everything happened.

That night, that wretched fucking night when my life turned upside down. It was something I couldn't forget. The scent of blood hanging heavy in the air. The screams from the humans being killed. The rally cry from the others coming to save them. The grief that felt like a fist to my chest when I saw my parents murdered.

It took a long time for me to come to terms with everything. I understood why the humans had done it. My family was out of control. They had to be stopped. I only wished there'd been another way to do it. I'd played that night over and over in my head. I was only ten, but I kept wondering if I could have done something, anything. Could have broken whatever spell they were under.

But we never found out if it was a spell or something else. Leven tried. He went to the mainland, talked with the locals including a mage. No one knew what drove the royal Ostin family to madness. And they looked. Leven would bring back newspapers with headlines of scientists searching for answers. Other vampire families offered them support. They feared it would happen to them. Finding an answer would benefit everyone. Too bad nothing ever came of it.

Leven kept me on this island, the Isle of Ostin as he called it, until I turned eighteen then he gave me the choice to travel with him to get what we needed. To see the town I'd left. He said no one would recognize me. I didn't look like a vampire. None of us did until they saw our fangs. But I couldn't do it. Couldn't bring myself to walk among humans like my family hadn't done something horrific. As far as the world knew, I died with the rest of them. Leven was the only one who knew I was alive. And now he was gone for too long on the supply run.

My pacing continued until I couldn't take it any longer and descended to the first floor of the castle. It was dark, just like the sea. Fortunately, it had electricity.

All royal vampires had magic within them. Each family possessed different skills. Mine could create light and darkness. Fire with a snap of my fingers. Bolts of lightning. Shadows and yes, fog that rolled over the water around the island. The magic didn't develop until we were thirteen years old.

This place was built hundreds of years ago by my father. Back then it was ostentatious. He was flaunting his wealth while other royals were beginning their rise. As time went on, this castle was left behind and fell into disarray, in favor of

The Ostin Heir

newer locations. That was until Leven brought me here the day everything changed.

We fixed it up the best we could with supplies he brought from the mainland. Before long, it felt better here. Not like home. The home I had was long gone when fire spread through it, along with everything I possessed.

The sound of a motor had me pausing my steps and sweeping my gaze out the window. A low light glowed from the bow as it approached. Only those in possession of my family's crest could see the island, enter it. My father liked to show off his wealth, but he also never wanted anyone to take it from him. After they were gone and Leven and I were here, I cloaked the island in darkness until Leven used a spell he purchased from a mage to hide it entirely. Ships were detoured around it. Planes never saw it, no matter how low they flew. This island was my sanctuary and prison.

The boat slid between the two tall towers that created the front of the unique castle. It formed a circle. In the center was a small area of deep water to dock the boat. There was sand which bled to stone that led to the castle itself. There was no grass here. No plants thrived without the rays of the sun. I liked it that way. I didn't need anything to bring me joy in my life. I didn't deserve it. Not after what my family did.

I walked through the hallway until I came to the door that exited to the center of the island. A man stood there, looking around. Most certainly not Leven. Quickly, I sank back to the shadows and used my magic to keep me hidden as I walked along the stone walls outside, trying to get a better look at the man who came here on Leven's boat.

He started walking toward the door I came from. That was when I struck. I moved in behind him, not letting him sense anything more than a slight breeze, until I stood with his back to my chest and reached in front to grip his throat.

"Where is Leven?" I seethed.

He tried to struggle out of my grasp, but it was of no use. I was much stronger than him. I tilted his head to the side and let my fangs descend so I could run them along the column of his neck. I hadn't drunk from a human in my life. Leven brought me food, fresh meats that he cooked rare, and I ate. He brought me blood in bags to drink to feed my needs. I didn't crave blood directly from a human since Leven was the only person I ever saw. But now, with this male's body pressed to mine, the blood pulsing through his veins, fuck, I was tempted.

"Tell me," I said harshly. "Or I'm going to suck every drop of life from your body."

He trembled in my hold. I didn't blame him. I had the power to snap his neck. To make his life a living hell if I chose to let him live. "Here," he coughed and handed me a crinkled piece of paper.

Even in the darkness I recognized the sticky note Leven liked to use. The things were all over his office. He told me on many occasions how bad his memory was, and these helped him remember.

Taking the note, I read the lines on it once then again. It was in his handwriting. The same that adorned the notes in his office.

Also, in the man's hand was something I'd recognize anywhere. It had my family crest on it after all. I snatched it from his grasp and shoved him roughly forward until he fell onto his hands and knees on the stone. He turned around to face me but stayed on the ground.

I stepped closer until I towered over him, holding up the note and necklace. "Who gave this to you?"

He rubbed at this throat. His voice was rough when he spoke. "A man on the pier. He disa-disappeared."

I brought myself over him until my feet were planted on

either side of his hips as I leaned down and fisted his shirt to bring him closer to my face. "You're lying." I could smell his fear but lies were nothing I could detect that way.

His eyes were wide, holding mine. "I'm n-not."

I shoved him back and tipped my head toward the sky. I roared out my anger and loss. The way the man shook, the fact that he was on the boat with this pendant and note, it was true. Leven was gone. Pain lanced through me more powerful than the day I lost everything. It had me walking into the castle on a warpath. Everything that lay in my way, I shredded. I didn't stop until I reached Leven's office. I wanted to destroy it, burn it all. I even had fire lit in my palm, but I couldn't do it. Couldn't destroy what Leven had made his.

On his desk was an envelope with my name on it. I sat on the leather chair and removed the letter within, my hands trembling as I did so.

Theo,

The time has come. You knew it was on the horizon. I've lived out my years. Drops of your blood extended my life, but I never wanted to be immortal like you.

You were the most important person in my life. I never got a chance to have children, but I considered you my son. I'm going to miss you with all my heart.

Don't be too hard on my replacement. I've known who he was for quite some time. He's a man who needs you as much as you need him. Hopefully, you don't kill him when he shows up with my boat.

Let him in, Son. Let him get to know the real you. Happiness could be right around the corner.

And don't make that face. This old man knows what he's talking about.

One day you're going to have to reveal your existence to the world. You can't hide in the castle forever.

You're not your parents. You're not your aunts, uncles, or cousins. You're Theo Ostin and you're meant for greatness.

I love you and I'll miss you.

Leven

Something wet dripped down onto the letter. Reaching up, I realized it was from me. I was crying. Son of a bitch, that man. He was like a father to me. Not related by blood, Leven was still family. He saved my life. Without him, I would have been killed. Though there were days early on when I wished I was. Leven told me I was meant for more. Reminded me of it whenever I needed to hear it.

He was a seer. One who became stronger when he wore the Ostin pendant around his neck. It amplified his abilities.

I dropped my head to my arms on the desk and cried. He was really gone. I knew it would happen soon. Leven said he felt it coming. A human could only live so long on drops of vampire blood. I offered to change him. To make him like me but he refused, saying that wasn't his destiny.

The only person in my life was dead.

A scuff of a shoe over stone snapped my head up, my eyes narrowing on the doorway. The figure there froze. I quickly wiped at my tears and pushed the chair forcefully so I could stand. It clattered to the floor.

"Don't move," I told him.

Out in the hallway, I used my magic to turn up the lights along the walls so I could take this man in. Or should I say boy because he was much younger than me.

Medium brown hair that was wavy and fell into his eyes of the same color. He was tall but I was taller by at least a few inches. He wasn't overly muscular but not frail either. Slender with clothes that had seen better days. I circled around him, taking in every aspect, even his scent, which reminded me of sandalwood, earthy, and rich.

"What's your name?" I asked when I was standing in front of him again.

His voice shook. "P-Paxton Huxley."

"How old are you?"

"Twenty-two."

"You know what I am."

His wide eyes held mine as he nodded.

"Do you know *who* I am?"

He shook his head. The pendant hadn't given me away.

"Let's keep it that way." I turned and walked up the hall. "Empty the boat!" I snapped. "The kitchen is on the other side of the castle. Find it!"

With that, I left him. No glancing back. Nothing but what was in front of me. I didn't stop until I was in my bedroom on the second floor with the door shut firmly behind me. I looked out onto the ocean. But that wasn't where I wanted my gaze.

I crossed the hallway into a spare bedroom and quickly peered out the window to find the man by the boat lifting bags of supplies Leven had bought. Leven made sure I had what I needed for the next two weeks. Enough time for me to lay down the rules for my new *guest*.

Though he wasn't a guest. He was mine now. Mine to do whatever I wanted him to.

3

PAXTON

My legs felt weak as I carried the bags to the kitchen. I had to search for it. On the first trip, I wandered around, hoping to stumble upon it. Eventually, I did.

It was a castle. In the middle of the ocean. With nothing surrounding it. And a vampire was the one who lived in it. I guessed the man I met on the pier used to live here too. The vampire was obviously upset hearing about the loss. I couldn't focus on his pain, not when the reality of who I was with filled me with fear.

I wanted to run. To get back in the boat and head to the pier. Back to safety. Though, did I ever feel safe there? Not after all I'd been through. I learned to adapt. To be smarter than those who came after me.

The world wasn't like it used to be many years ago. It changed when the vampires were killed. I'd never known any different, but I read enough to understand how it used to be. Happy. Vibrant. Everything life should be. Until it wasn't.

There were good parts of the world, of Delaware. Too bad I didn't live in one of them. I had to prop a dresser against my apartment door whenever I was inside to prevent my neighbors from coming in during the middle of the night and taking something from me I never wanted to give. But I couldn't afford to move. I barely had enough to buy cheap packets of noodles to eat. Adapt, that was what I did. Learned to protect myself. And yet, I somehow got myself into what might be a worse situation.

Who this vampire was, I wish I knew. I had so many questions that would go unanswered until I had the balls to ask him. Because right now, I was terrified. If I did what he asked, would he let me go? Shit, what was I going back to? Fending off being assaulted every time I came and left my apartment? Maybe it was better if I stayed here and became a meal for the vampire. At least it would be over quickly.

When we learned about them, we were told they didn't bite or drink from random humans. Yet, that fear sank into all our minds as children. How could it not? Vampires drank blood. The teachers told us they did it from each other. That they could eat human food too. But there were still movies out there —fiction based on these royal families—where they did drink from humans. Because movie writers liked to romanticize them. I could understand the appeal when they did that. But that wasn't the reality I was faced with.

The castle was unlike anything I'd ever seen, even on TV. It was dark everywhere. The kitchen had black wooden cabinets with black stone countertops. The floor was a deep slate color in the same stone that made up the walls. At least it was a variation of the color. Not completely shrouded in darkness. But it wasn't all bad. There were some modern appliances plus the expensive-looking coffee maker and the microwave.

The rooms I passed when I went to and from the boat all had the doors closed, leaving the mystery of what was behind them intact. There were boxes I brought inside that I wasn't sure where the contents went, so I stacked them in a corner. I wasn't going to seek out the master of the manor to ask for direction.

When I got back to the boat for the last bag, I wondered how it knew to come here. It was a miracle I figured out how to start it. I'd never been in a boat before. If I needed to actually drive it, I would have been floating out in the middle of nowhere, not sure what to do. But the boat came right here. To this tiny bit of sea that came in through the narrow channel from the Atlantic.

I studied the boat for a moment too long because a harsh voice behind me caused me to jump and turn, the contents of the bag spilling out and rolling along the sand. Blood oranges, passionfruit, kiwi, and mangoes. This bag was full of them and other fruit. Of course, only the ones that could roll managed to escape.

Placing the bag down, I began to collect the fruit. Some I had to wade slightly into the water to grab, soaking my shoes which had the soles held together with duct tape and a prayer. From the looks of the inside of the castle, I wasn't sure if this would be an upgrade to the job I already had or not. Thinking of that, if I didn't come in tomorrow, I would surely be fired.

Carefully, I put the collected fruit back into the bag, picked it up, and stood straight. I'd let this man see enough of my fear when I first got here. I knew better than to show my weaknesses. Had he not caught me off guard, I would have been better equipped to handle him.

Or not. He was a vampire and I... wasn't.

We stared at each other. I finally got the chance to take him in. Dark hair that was cut close on the sides and longer on top. He didn't have it styled, more pushed back from his face by a brush or his fingers. His eyes were like onyx orbs, holding me to the spot. I couldn't tell if they were a dark color that blended with his pupils or if they were the same solid color. He had a bit of scruff with a chiseled jaw beneath it. Broad shoulders. A long-sleeved shirt covered him from neck to wrists. Dark blue denim clothed his legs, his feet were bare. And there was a pendant around his neck that looked like the one he took from me.

It was shaped in an oval in a light brown. There was an O carved close to the edge in black. In the middle of the O was a flame done in a medium orange at the top. Below it was a wave in a deep gray flipped upside down. They touched at the center. I'd never seen anything like it until the man on the pier showed it to me.

"Where's mine?" I asked him. It was bold of me to do so but it was given to me.

The vampire stepped close, less than a foot separated us. I could smell the salty air on him. Yes, we were outside, but it was amplified when he was near. He stared down at me, easily four inches taller. "Yours?" His voice was deep. Within it was plenty of menace.

"It was given to me by... by..."

"You don't even know his name."

"He never told me." I stood my ground. Kept my spine straight, no matter how much I wanted to shrink before him.

"The man who gave you this," he dangled the one I had from his finger, "was the only family I had. He took care of me since I was a child. And I didn't even get a chance to say goodbye. But you did. You were there. And I bet you had no clue what a great man was before you. Leven. That was his name."

I swallowed, hard.

"Say it!" he roared.

"Leven."

"Louder!"

"Leven!"

"Now remember it. Because he bestowed this gift upon you.

My family's crest on this pendant. And with it comes responsibilities. Ones you can't begin to fathom. You'll learn or you'll die. Put the rest of this shit away and cook me a steak. Rare." He dropped the pendant into my hand before being swallowed up by the shadows and disappearing into the castle.

The pendant glowed in my hand again. Just as it did the first time I held it, not lasting long. I didn't understand what it meant, but it was obvious it was special. I slipped it over my head.

His words stuck with me. His family's crest. It jogged loose a memory from school. One about the crests that the royals each had, not just here but all around the world. And...

No. It couldn't be.

I studied the pendant. Went through the royal surnames in my head of the families who resided in the United States.

Asteria.

Kade.

Monroe.

Xander.

Each started with a different letter. Each had a different crest.

This one started with an O.

Ostin.

Holy fucking shit.

"But you were all killed," I said aloud, only there was no one to hear me.

If what I thought was true, he was a member of the Ostin family. A royal. He survived when no one thought anyone did. And I was standing on the sand by his castle.

I thought back. Tried to remember other things they taught us, but I came up empty. I was never a fanatic like some of the others. I didn't go vampire crazy when I learned about them. To me, it was just another part of history I had to learn so I could do well and move up to the next grade. That was my goal. Never fall behind. I didn't want to be in school longer than I had to. It wasn't a fun place for me.

Once the awe of what I just uncovered floated away, I was left with a sense of dread. This family of vampires murdered humans. Did that mean this one would kill me? He hadn't yet. He could be waiting or maybe he wouldn't do it at all.

The bag slipped a little in my arms, reminding me he told me to make him dinner. I bolted toward the kitchen and put the fruit away. In the fridge, I grabbed a thick rib eye steak and looked around. There were ovens. An electric stovetop. I didn't see a place to grill outside. Broiling in the oven or searing it on the stove were my options. He did say rare. Searing won.

I searched in the cabinets until I found a large pan and turned the burner on. There was some olive oil I used to drizzle into the pan. I'd never made a steak before. Couldn't afford to buy one. Hopefully, I didn't ruin it.

The pan heated and I added the steak to it. Did he want it seasoned? I had no idea. There were spices in the pantry, so I used some of them, hoping I was doing the right thing. What the hell did I know about cooking steak for a vampire? At least he wasn't coming to me for my blood as a meal.

The room next to the kitchen had a long, wooden dining table that sat twenty. I counted. I took the plate to the head of the table, unsure what else to do. Then I grabbed a glass of water since the only other drinks were orange juice, coffee, and a bottle of wine that had a layer of dust on it.

I stood near the table and waited. He didn't show. More time ticked by. Eventually, I stepped out into the hallway and looked in both directions only to be met by silence.

"Mr. Ostin! Dinner's ready!" Was that how I was supposed to address him? He was a royal vampire, but he wasn't a royal anything to me, except maybe he was since I was currently trapped on his island. The only people the royals led were the ones in their families.

He appeared, walking toward me from around a corner. "Since you've already worked out who I am, thanks to the crest, you may call me Theo." His tone wasn't as harsh this time but there was still an edge to it. "Mr. Ostin was my father."

"My parents gave me up when I was a baby," I rambled, not sure what to say. "I never knew them. Years later, my father died of a drug overdose. So did my mother." I shrugged. If he shared and I did, hopefully we could get past him yelling at me and actually have a conversation. "Not everyone wants a reminder of a past."

He glared and stepped around me to go into the dining room.

So much for a conversation.

4

THEO

What was he playing at, telling me about his lineage? If he was searching for sympathy, he should look elsewhere.

The scent of the cooking meat drifted down the hall to me, but I had kept to the shadows to see what he would do. Paxton. I should start using his name. He was going to be here a while. It wasn't like I could send him back and tell him to pick someone else to assist me. I couldn't interview anyone. Leven made this choice.

As I took a seat, I immediately thought about the last meal I ate. The one Leven had prepared. It wasn't that I didn't know how to cook. He taught me. Wanted me to learn how to do everything for myself. But he enjoyed it, so he made my meals.

The first bite was flavorful. The cracked pepper worked well. Not that I would tell Paxton that. He had to earn my praise. Do more than this. I could almost hear Leven's voice in my head, telling me it was a start and to go easy on him.

I sighed and looked down at the steak. It was rare like I asked. Seasoned, which I didn't but was pleased with. Paxton was thrown at me. If what he said was true, and he had no reason to lie, Leven didn't tell him more than what was on the note. If he did, I imagined Paxton would have run in the other direction. No one would want anything to do with an Ostin.

Paxton didn't think I'd heard him before, but I did. He had thought my family was all dead. Yet here I was, eating steak by myself in a castle that was as dark as my soul. And Paxton was still standing in the hallway. Did he cook something for himself?

I shook my head. Not my problem. He could eat. Only I never told him he could have any food here.

"Paxton!"

He rushed into the room.

"Don't forget to feed yourself. I don't want you withering away. Just don't eat my fucking steaks."

"Okay. Do you need anything else?"

I looked up and held his eyes. I was young when my father was killed but he instilled a lot of lessons in me. He wasn't a hard man. He was loving with me and my mother. I remembered everything he taught me. We were royals after all, and we should behave as such. That meant holding eye contact. Using it to intimidate the one you were focused on if you so desired. If the way Paxton trembled said anything, it was working.

"Your bedroom is on the second floor, above the kitchen," I told him. When he was putting away the items Leven purchased, I went into the spare bedrooms near mine and wondered how much preparation Leven put into this. I had no doubt he did a fair amount of research on Paxton.

In the room beside mine was a closet full of clothes—Paxton-sized to be precise. I grabbed them and hauled them down the hallway to the other side of the castle, along with the clothes in the dresser: socks, underwear, and anything else he might need. I wasn't having this man stay near me for a multitude of reasons.

I didn't know him. Leven might have thought he could be

The Ostin Heir

trusted, but I didn't know any such thing. I had to make sure he wouldn't stake me in my sleep. With him far away, I'd hear him coming. He couldn't tread lightly if his life depended on it. I'd heard how he walked through the castle.

But that wasn't the main reason. This one I would only admit to myself.

The thought of what happened to my family hung heavy over me. Having never known what caused it to happen, I was worried the same fate would befall me. And I didn't want that. Paxton was here. Leven approved. I had to keep him alive, at the very least, or that man would find a way to haunt me even if ghosts weren't real.

Paxton was still standing there, waiting for more.

I bit back a curse. I didn't want to keep talking to him. "You didn't bring clothes with you, did you?"

He shook his head. "All I have is what's in my pockets." He emptied them to show me his wallet, keys, and a phone.

I hadn't left the castle, but I knew about modern technology. Another thing Leven made sure of. I was homeschooled by him to the best of his abilities, educated, and kept up with the times like any other royal out there. He said if I ever went back to the mainland, he didn't want me shocked by how much it changed.

"Leven saw to that. Anything you need should be in there, including a letter he left you. Eat and go to sleep. I expect breakfast when the sun rises." With that, I shooed him away. He didn't hesitate to bolt from the room.

That damn letter for Paxton was sealed. I was curious about what it said but knew better than to open it.

I ate the rest of the steak, taking my time. No matter how much food I ate, it didn't sate my hunger, merely dulled it. Once a month, Leven brought me blood. He would get it from the mage he knew. Her name was Novus. She had no idea I was alive, but nonetheless always asked Leven who he was purchasing things for. Leven would tell her it was a low-level vampire he befriended.

The blood helped for a bit. Then the hunger would begin again. My parents used to feed from each other. As a child, I didn't have this thirst for blood yet. That didn't develop until I was seventeen. By then Leven had already secured me blood. I was worried I'd go mad when I drank, but he reminded me vampires drank all the time and never went crazy. That fear was always there though. That worry of turning into my family.

I shook the thoughts away and took my plate toward the kitchen. I didn't expect Paxton to clean after me too. Leven never did.

Shit. I had to stop comparing them. They weren't the same nor would they ever be. I still couldn't be completely disrespectful. My dishes were just that, mine to clean.

Stepping into the kitchen, which I thought would be empty by now, I came to a stop. There before me was Paxton, bent over, looking into the pantry for something. His ass high in the air.

Something stirred inside me. Something I only felt in the privacy of my bedroom because I damn sure wasn't going to discuss it with Leven.

My dick began to harden, becoming painful where it pressed against my jeans. I must have made a sound because Paxton stood up and turned around. I moved to the sink, hoping he didn't see what his presence did to me.

The plate and silverware became my sole focus as I washed, dried, and put them away. When I turned around, he was gone. Paxton could be quiet after all.

I leaned back against the sink and scrubbed my hands over my face. I hadn't been attracted to anyone ever. That was what happened when I never left and the only person here was someone who wasn't in a million years going to be who I desired.

Paxton didn't appeal to me the other times I saw him. Yes, I recognized he was good-looking, but I didn't get hard. I guessed that partially answered the question I always had about if I was gay, straight, bisexual, or something else. So far, I was attracted to men. Or maybe it was just Paxton. I wasn't sure. The only way to find out was to go to the mainland and that wasn't an option.

We had electricity here, thanks to my father's magic and mine, plus the spell of a mage to make it everlasting. My father built this castle and injected his magic into it. I added more when I needed to. But I didn't have the capability to create an internet service. Nor would cell phones work here. Too far off the grid, as Leven liked to say.

Instead of going to my room for the night, I decided to climb the stairs in one of the towers and take them to the top until I was out in the open, with a view of the fog rolling around the castle above the ocean. The salty air greeted me like an old friend. No matter where my thoughts took me, how deep within myself I withdrew, I could come here and just be. Breathe in the air. Listen to the waves. Pretend I wasn't alone. I used to have Leven and now had Paxton.

Paxton.

My dick stirred at the thought of him. Just what I needed. I couldn't walk around the castle hard all the time.

Reaching down, I palmed myself. There wasn't anyone who could see me. The island was cloaked. And Paxton was in his room, probably too afraid to explore the castle.

My dick hardened quickly under my touch, so I undid my jeans, reached inside my boxer briefs and pulled it out. Once I got off, maybe I could go back to the way things were. When I only fantasized in my room. When there wasn't temptation residing in the castle with me. But Paxton wasn't going anywhere. Hopefully, this was all I needed to get him out of my system.

Leaning against the low wall, I fisted myself and used my precum to coat my dick so my hand could glide smoothly over my flesh. I moaned and my eyes slipped closed; my head tipped back. I just felt.

Stroke after stroke, I kept going, bringing myself closer to the brink, while my other hand went to my balls to play with them. I'd never tried putting even a finger in my ass so why was I thinking about it now? Or it wasn't my finger there but Paxton's. I couldn't think like this, yet my brain was latched on to this vision of him on his knees for me. My dick in his mouth while he rubbed past my balls and moved until his finger tapped my hole.

I cried out and hunched forward as cum shot from me in ropes. My body trembled, my eyes stayed closed, and my vision filled with nothing but a fantasy of Paxton.

That wavy hair of his falling into his eyes as he doubled his efforts to suck every last drop from me. His finger breached me to the knuckle.

Holy shit, it wouldn't stop. I turned to lean my hip against the wall for more support. My knees threatened to give out. One last shot came from my dick before I couldn't take it any longer and had to let go, so I could brace my hand on the wall. My hand that had cum on it.

I stood there, breathing hard, wondering what the hell I was going to do now because that idea of getting Paxton out of my head wasn't going to work. If anything, I wanted him more. Especially on his knees for me. Like I'd read about in books.

I had a whole library of various genres. Non-fiction and fiction. Fantasy and contemporary. Romance. Those were the ones I'd read the most. Probably because it was something so foreign to me. I remembered that my parents loved each other, but actual romance? I hadn't experienced it. And in those books, there was a heaping dose of sex.

Leven would bring me anything he could find that he thought might interest me. He didn't stick to a man with a woman. He branched out, saying he hoped it would help me find what I was truly interested in. It didn't. I loved every book, regardless of the genders of those inside the pages.

But now with Paxton in my home. The way his ass was in the air. The vision I conjured up of him bringing me pleasure. I wanted to experience that in real life. I wouldn't dare let myself get that close to Paxton though. I didn't trust him. He feared me. I also didn't trust myself.

5

PAXTON

The room was more than I'd ever had before. There was a king-sized, four-poster bed in a deep cherrywood. The bedding was a muted sky blue. Not dreary like the rest of the castle but not overly bright either.

It wasn't hard to find it. The other rooms up here had furniture in them, but they were bare otherwise. No curtains. No bedding.

The dresser and nightstands matched the bed. Within the dresser I found various types of underwear: briefs, boxers, boxer briefs. There were many types of socks from wool to dress. Undershirts. T-shirts. Shorts. Then in the closet, which wasn't quite a walk-in, since this was an old castle, were a few suits, a tuxedo, jeans, collared shirts, and more. This must have cost a small fortune.

I took time trying on various things and they all fit perfectly. Theo said Leven selected me, which meant he must have been watching me. It was creepy if I was being honest, but at the same time, I understood. He couldn't have just anyone come here and work for a royal vampire. One no one knew existed.

Picking up the letter on the dresser, I saw my name written across it in black ink. There were two pieces of paper within, as well as a credit card with my name on it and a boating license with my picture and information on it, which was mind-boggling on its own. One paper was a list of items Leven normally picked up in Delaware and where to get them. The other was a handwritten letter on lined paper in the same black ink.

Paxton,

By now you're getting settled into the Isle of Ostin. This is a magical place, but you might not see it as such. You were tricked into this and for that, I'm sorry. I had to take care of Theo though. I doubt he's told you much about himself so let me fill you in a little.

Theo was only ten years old when I dragged him through the streets and out toward the boat his family kept nearby. Everyone was being killed. I couldn't let that happen to him as well. He fought me, didn't want to leave them. And it wasn't easy for me to go either but I had promised his father, many years ago, that I would always look after his son.

This island you're on, Theo hasn't left it since. He's afraid of what will happen if he does. That he'll end up like his family. That he'll hurt others. We never found out why they did what they did, but it's always there in Theo's mind. Haunting him.

I doubt he came off warm to you. He's likely upset by my loss and how I didn't tell him of my plan with you. He'll come around though.

Theo is a good man. He's caring and honest. Would do anything within his power for me. But I could never get him to leave. Maybe you'll have better luck.

There's more for him in this world. It won't be an easy path if he does make his presence known to everyone. But he'll be able to do it with you by his side.

Be patient with him. He'll get angry. He'll snap at you. It will feel personal, and it might be at first, but it won't later. Theo has a hard time expressing his feelings. Just keep in mind that he wasn't brought up like most others. He's lived a solitary life for far too long, with only me as a friend and a father figure.

I also apologize for invading your privacy. I needed to find someone to take my spot. Someone I could trust with Theo. To treat him well and be gentle. Once I found you, I knew there would be no one else. I did more research on you every time I came to the mainland.

Hopefully, you can understand why I didn't tell you this when I finally spoke to you. Would you have believed me? Jumped at the chance to come here? My guess would be no. I said what I had to, so you'd come.

This life before you won't be simple. It will be filled with trying times, an array of emotions, but if you can win Theo over, you'll have someone who will become your best friend.

You've both been through a lot in life and have more in common than you realize. Yes, Theo is a vampire, but beneath that, he's a man who missed out on so much.

Take care of each other, Paxton. I wish I could be there to guide you, but I have a feeling you're going to do better than you think.

With my deepest thanks and apologies,

Leven

I fell back on the bed and looked up at the ceiling. My mind spun. Some things confirmed, others surprising. Once I met Theo and realized who he was, I didn't think I was just anybody. I was chosen. Leven wouldn't have let someone who he didn't know come here. Trust his pendant with.

But the other things about Theo... Things I wouldn't have guessed. Was there really someone else hiding behind that angry exterior? I got a glimpse of it. But nothing to solidify he was just hurt right now.

The Ostin Heir

I sighed. This wasn't going to be easy. Not that anything had been since I arrived. Winning Theo over to think of me as something more than the man who took his friend's spot was going to be difficult.

Leven said Theo had never left the island since he was brought here. What must that have been like for Theo? Being pulled from everything he knew. Did he see his parents murdered? I shook my head to try and rid the dark thoughts. Though dark was where I resided most of the time. My life wasn't full of happiness.

I sat up and decided to go exploring a little bit at this end of the castle. I was only slightly worried Theo would appear and yell at me for not staying in my room. I'd deal with that if it happened.

The hallway only went so far before it ended in a tower. Must have been the one with the tall spire at the top. They flanked either side of the small channel I passed through in the boat. I walked the opposite way, this time going in each bedroom and looking around rather than merely glancing inside.

The rooms were clean, not dusty like I'd expect them to be since no one lived in them. They were just bare. The windows on this side looked out into the center of the island where the boat was. I was almost halfway down the corridor, giving me a view of the channel that led inside too.

Looking down at the beach, I wondered if Theo ever went out there and dug his toes into the sand like I had done on Desolate. The beach wasn't bright and cheery, but it was still sand. Still ocean. The view out my bedroom windows was of the ocean, vast and nothing in sight beyond. I knew it was there —Delaware—but it wasn't seen.

I found the lever to unlock the window, which was more modern than I'd expected. The glass was thick and clear. The hinges not battered from the salt in the air. Magic, I reminded myself. I was sure that had something to do with it.

The sea breeze came into the sparse room, immediately putting me at ease like it did at Desolate. Maybe those inky fingers of sand I always thought were reaching out for help were actually trying to get to the island where they belonged. The small beach town knew Theo was out here.

No, that sounded ridiculous. It was a town not a living, breathing thing.

A sound drew my gaze up toward the top of the castle. Even at night, I could make out the spires reaching high into the sky. The moon was out. Not enough to cast any bright light. It was dimmed like the sun was during the day. Everything more muted here.

I was still able to make out the silhouette of Theo on the top of a tower. Not the one with a spire. This one was open to the air. There must be a walkway up there or something. I didn't know much about castles or how they were built. What I'd learned since being here was the extent of my knowledge.

What Theo was doing, or what I thought he was doing, I knew very well.

The moan that left his lips had me hard in an instant. I'd known since I was fourteen that I was gay. While Theo was a vampire, he was also very attractive.

He cried out before turning and giving me a better view. I couldn't help but reach down and rub my hand over my dick. I hadn't been with anyone in a year. Hadn't found a man I trusted since then.

My eyes stayed glued to Theo. I only watched him a little while longer before easing back and closing the window, which was thankfully silent. I would have died a thousand deaths if the hinges squeaked loudly.

I made a point to ignore my dick back in my room. The

door was shut. I was in my own space. That didn't mean I was ready to start jerking off to the man who currently held my life in the palm of his hand.

Theo had the ability to kill me. He was a vampire after all. Would he? That was anyone's guess. By the letter Leven left, I was hoping my heart would continue beating. Theo needed me. Without me, he couldn't get the food he needed. The blood that was on Leven's list.

A mage. I had to visit a mage to get that. I'd never met one before. They were mysterious and a lot wasn't known about them. They kept to themselves.

I was grateful Leven left directions on how to find the mage. I'd be nervous when the time came to visit her. At least I didn't have to go for a month. Leven had just gone before he vanished in front of me. I found the blood when I was putting away the food. I almost threw up at the sight but managed not to. Knowing what vampires drank and seeing it in a bag were two very different things.

As I lay in bed with the lights out and one of the windows open slightly, so I could hear the ocean lapping the rocks below, I stared into the darkness above me, wondering what tomorrow would bring. I was here for at least two weeks. When those weeks were up, I had to go back to the coast to shop for Theo. I could stay and never return. Could pretend like all of this didn't happen. Could I do that to Theo? He wasn't nice to me. He didn't treat me with respect. I could understand it to an extent.

Two weeks. In that amount of time, he needed to show me there was something else to him besides being an asshole. Something that would make me want to come back once I left.

My life in Delaware sucked. I didn't enjoy it, but it was mine. And here I was in a situation not of my choosing. Well, I did get on the boat.

Things could always be worse. I had to keep telling myself

that. I was alive. Had a new job apparently. Plus, I was the only person in the world who knew a member of the Ostin family was alive.

6

THEO

The clock sat on the nightstand beside my bed. I never looked at it. Leven said I should know what time it was, but what was the point when I never left here? I didn't need to wake at any certain time. I had nowhere to be except for breakfast.

My stomach growled. Food was required. Maybe some blood.

I got out of bed and pulled on a pair of jeans and a T-shirt. On the ground level, the scent of bacon reached me. My mouth began to water. It could have been the food. It could have also been the fact that Paxton was the one cooking it. The man I thought about as I brought myself to orgasm last night not once, but three times. Because when I came into my room for the night, I couldn't sleep so I jerked off again. I grabbed a book. Read for a bit. Jerked off once more before sleep finally claimed me.

I welcomed it. It was only there I found solace. I didn't dream. It was a relaxing experience. One that helped me get ready for the day.

Dreams were something my parents spoke of. My cousins. But I didn't understand them until I read more because I never had one. That didn't mean my imagination was absent too. That obviously existed since I could picture Paxton on his knees.

My imagination was all I had. I'd never been with a man or woman before. Never known an intimate touch like I'd read so many times in books. Would I welcome it? Crave it? Give in and let someone else take over for a bit? Or would I be the one dominating? I had no idea. No experience to base it on.

I froze in place when I entered the dining room. The table was set. For two. One at either end.

Leven ate with me of course. We had a good relationship. We talked. Got along well. Paxton and I didn't know each other. I should take the time to understand him. Learn about him. But doing so would mean he'd want to know about me and there was only so much I could share. I certainly couldn't lay my vulnerabilities out there. That would give him too much access to me.

There was already a high stack of pancakes on the table as well as a bowl of scrambled eggs.

Paxton came in with a plate of bacon and a bottle of the blueberry syrup I loved so much. How much did he know? The letter Leven left for him; I should have read it. I didn't know what was said about me in it. Was the syrup in there or was this a guess?

"Good morning," Paxton greeted. He didn't smile, yet wasn't terse with his words. Before I could respond, he continued, "I wasn't sure what time you normally got up. I was about to come and get you. You saved me from doing so." He put the plate and syrup on the table. "Eat." He jutted his chin toward the food then turned to grab his plate and fill it.

I wanted to snap at him and remind him he wasn't to order me around, but I had to try to get to know him. He was going to be staying with me for who knew how long. Deciding not to say a thing, I followed suit and filled my plate.

When we were both seated, it felt like there was a chasm between us for as long as the table was. I could sense Paxton's eyes on me every now and then, although I didn't glance up. Didn't want to meet them. It was rude. I should say thank you, but the words wouldn't come from my mouth. Instead, I kept putting more food in it.

My plate was empty; my stomach still growled. The food wasn't enough. I took my plate to the kitchen and went back to grab the others since Paxton was done too. Without a word, he followed me into the kitchen and stood beside me as I washed the dishes so he could dry them and put them away.

It was... odd.

When we were done, I braced my hands on the counter and dropped my head. I needed blood but didn't think Paxton would react too kindly to me drinking it in front of him. I was trying to be courteous. Only, he didn't take the hint and leave me alone.

"Are you in pain?" he asked.

My shoulders tensed more than they already were. If I'd had my fill of blood and was at my full strength, I would have broken the countertop with the force I was gripping it with.

"Theo, I can help you. Just tell me what you need."

I spun quickly. Gripped him by his throat and pulled him close until our noses touched. He should have left me be. But he hadn't. He apparently gave a fuck about how I was feeling, and I didn't know what to do with that.

His vein pulsed under my fingers. "What I need?" I asked. My thumb stroked the side of his neck. "You have a body full of it." I could only hold his eyes for so long before moving my face and dipping it down. I dragged my nose along his neck. "I can smell your fear, Paxton. Even if I couldn't, the trembling of your body would give you away." My tongue snaked out and I dared to taste just a fraction of his skin. Goddamn, he was salty and sweet. A heady combination.

"I-I put blood in the refrigerator. The second one meant for it. I could get you some."

My dick hardened at the proximity to Paxton, but it wasn't his fear I was getting off on. It was his taste. The silkiness of his skin. The rough stubble along his jaw when I nuzzled my cheek to his. I couldn't resist grinding against him. A moan tore up my throat. I'd never pressed myself to another's body. Never felt that heat, that lust, coming from them.

Paxton was hard too, the evidence of it against my hip. "Th-Theo?"

I pulled back with a curse and roughly shoved him aside, so I could open the door to the fridge he was referring to. I picked up a pouch and tore the top off with my teeth. The moment the crimson liquid hit my taste buds; my body came alive in ways it only did when I was feeding like this.

The blood trickled over my tongue, down my throat with every swallow. It coated my stomach and was absorbed into my body. This was what I needed. Too bad it was cold and not fresh from a vein. I couldn't do that though. Not after everything.

Paxton made a noise as I was licking the pouch clean. I turned and found him staring at me with wide eyes.

My tongue licked over my bottom lip, sure to reach the corner and gather any blood I missed. "You knew I was a vampire. Knew I drank blood when you unpacked it. Yet, you stand here and stare at me like I'm a freak on display. Like I'm about to lose control and dive for your vein. I might tease you, but I would never drink from you." I threw the pouch into the garbage. I'd have to handle that later today. Incinerate it since it wasn't like there was a boat that came by to collect it.

"I..." He swallowed. "What time do you want lunch?"

"What?" I asked, confused. That wasn't what I expected him to say. I figured he'd run back to his room. Only appearing later when I needed him. But he stood his ground, no matter how scared he was. His fear still hung in the air with a bitter scent.

"I don't know what you do around here all day. You need to eat." He glanced over to the garbage where the pouch of empty blood sat within.

I looked down and noticed he was no longer hard. Not that I thought he would be. He'd seen me nourish my dark side. The one that craved blood but never gave in to searching for another vampire to drink from. My eyes drifted back up his body until I met his.

"We're going to be here together," he said. "Shouldn't we get along? At least a little? There's no one else here. Just the two of us."

"You want to be friends?" I cocked an eyebrow. The single friend I'd had was Leven.

He shrugged.

I stepped into his space again but this time not touching him. I couldn't resist him. Not when I had this fresh power pumping through my body. Not when he was close, yet felt completely unattainable. "And what if I wanted more?" I was bolder with my words than with my thoughts. I couldn't let him know I was afraid of his rejection and his continued fear of me.

"Like what?" He tipped his head back to peer up at me. I loved the height difference between us.

My hands found his hips. My dick hadn't softened. I pressed it to him. "I think you know."

"I haven't been with anyone in a while. I don't trust easily. There have been some men who..." Damn this man and his half thoughts.

"Who?" I prompted.

"Who took advantage of me," he rushed out. "Who broke

into my apartment. Who raped me. I put a stop to it happening again. Protected myself."

"What?" I bellowed. "Someone did that to you?" White-hot rage rose in me. I'd never been so angry in my life. "Who are they? I'll kill them." I hadn't left this island in a long time, but I'd seriously contemplate it if Paxton gave me names.

A gentle hand pressed to my chest, right over my rapidly beating heart. "I handled it. And many months later started dating someone, but that didn't last either."

"And here I am practically forcing myself on you." I released him and took three measurable steps back, disgusted with myself.

Paxton didn't let me go far. He advanced toward me until my waist hit the counter. "If I would have told you to stop, would you?"

"Yes." I didn't need to think about that. I might be a monster, a son of a monster, but I couldn't hurt Paxton that way. Even in my fantasies, he was willing.

"Then I trust you."

"You don't know what you're saying. You shouldn't put your trust in me. Look around you, Paxton. I have nothing to offer."

"I haven't been here twenty-four hours and this job is already better than the one I had back home."

"What did you do?" Guilt ate at me. He gave up everything to come here without knowing he wouldn't be returning for weeks. Though I wasn't the only one at fault. Leven was too, except he wasn't here for me to bitch at about what he did to Paxton.

"I cleaned offices at night. It sucked but it paid, and I didn't have to talk to anyone while I did it."

"Is there someone back there who will miss you?" He'd said he didn't have parents and hadn't been with anyone intimately recently.

He shook his head. "No. Leven must have known that. I don't think he'd approach a person with a family to come here. I was alone."

I wanted to take him in my arms and tell him he never would be again. That as long as I was alive, I'd be here for him. But I couldn't and didn't. That would be too much and surely give him more reason to run from me, given the chance.

Instead, I said, "I'm sorry. For you being coerced into coming here, as well as for the shit you dealt with when you were home. I will strive to do better than I have been."

"You don't have to."

"I do."

It was important to me that Paxton didn't see me as the monster I thought I was. Or like the men who treated him terribly. I couldn't go on behaving like I was. I had to change. If I wanted to be better, I had to behave like it. And that started now.

7

PAXTON

Something changed that morning in the kitchen. Something that had Theo treating me better. I'd lie if I said I didn't miss the commanding presence he had. He still showed me glimpses of it then seemed to realize what he was doing and backed off.

It had been a week since then. A week of us talking but never saying too much. Neither of us offered up more information about us personally but still found things to talk about. And I had a week to decide if, when I left for supplies, I was going to come back.

Part of me knew I would. The part who had seen the other side of Theo. The kind one. The one who hated how he treated me. Who wanted revenge for what those men did to me.

But the other part knew this was a dangerous slope I was on. Could I really live here the rest of my life? Isolated on this island, only leaving once every two weeks for a short period of time?

It was a lot to consider. So much so, it kept me up at night.

I felt off all day. I was dizzy when I woke up, which came and went as the day went on. I got through breakfast and lunch but by dinner, I knew this was a migraine settling in. I couldn't afford health insurance back home and didn't have anything here to take. Ibuprofen or acetaminophen. They weren't the best for treating migraines but maybe they could take the edge off. I did see some soda in the pantry that had caffeine in it. The combination worked for me in the past. But most of all, I needed to lie down. To close the curtains. Make the room dark and sleep it off. I had to tell Theo though. I didn't want him showing up for dinner and seeing the table bare.

I was halfway to his room, not sure where he'd be, when another wave of dizziness hit me, and I had to reach out to grip the wall so I didn't fall over. A pained groan left my lips as the searing sharpness in my head intensified. It was like an ice pick in my eye.

"Paxton?" I heard from a distance then the sound of Theo moving quickly, getting louder the closer he got. "Paxton?"

I looked up and there he was, walking toward me with a look in his eyes I hadn't seen before. He was worried.

Rushing forward, he stopped when he was near me and put his hand under my chin to tip my face toward his. "What's wrong?"

"I've got a migraine. I won't be able to make you dinner."

"I don't care about that. I can cook for myself. In fact, I should be."

"I like doing it, but I can't tonight."

"What will make you feel better?"

"Sleep. A dark room."

He nodded.

The next thing I knew, I was swept off my feet and the room spun once more. I gripped onto Theo for dear life as he started walking up the hallway. I swallowed thickly, begging my stomach to keep down what I had eaten earlier. I didn't want to puke all over him.

We went up a flight of stairs all the while my eyes remained closed. I was afraid if I opened them, everything would spin again.

I was carefully placed down on a bed but knew immediately it wasn't mine. The scent of the sea air mixed with spice that was unique to Theo hit me the second my head laid on the pillow. He'd brought me to his room. But why? Mine had curtains. It would be dark enough. I'd never even seen his room. I avoided it and Leven's office and old bedroom, not wanting to anger Theo or invade his privacy.

I didn't ask why. Didn't know if he'd answer me truthfully. So, I burrowed into the blankets and forced my mind to turn off so I could sleep. If I kept trying to figure Theo out, that wouldn't happen.

I stirred awake. The first thing I felt was the pain in my head. It had moved and was now in my temple. Just as intense but it was roving. I blinked and saw the time on a digital alarm clock. Four o'clock. Must be in the morning. I groaned when I rolled over, changing sides. I tried to not sleep on the side the migraine was on but sometime during the night I shifted positions.

I pulled the blankets up and slid down a little, loving the luxurious feel of the bed. I remembered I was in Theo's room. Remembered what happened earlier.

I opened my eyes again and saw him sitting there beside the bed, the lights weren't on but it was him.

"I found some medicine," he said in the softest voice I'd ever heard him use. "Leven had it in the bathroom. He stocked it for you. I didn't realize he'd done so." That didn't make any sense. The bathroom I'd been using was bare.

"Where?" I asked, my throat a little dry.

"Just down the hall here. He had given you a room close to mine, but I moved everything the day you arrived. I was angry. I apologize. I didn't know he filled the bathroom too. I don't use it. Have my own attached here."

"The medicine?" I couldn't dissect his words right now.

"It's ibuprofen. Says it helps with pain."

I untucked my arm from the blankets and held it out, palm up. Theo dropped two pills into it. I sat up slightly, not liking what it did to my head. He handed me a glass and I quickly swallowed them down before tucking myself back in.

If Theo said anything else, I didn't hear him. I dropped back off to sleep

---

The next time I awoke, I felt much better. I sat up, testing movement to make sure the dizziness and pain were gone. I had neither so I opened my eyes and looked around the room. Theo wasn't here. The room was still bathed in darkness.

My bladder made itself known. I got out of bed and shuffled over the cold stone floor to the bathroom. I was done worrying about invading his space. He put me in his bed; I was using his bathroom.

One step into the room, I turned on the light, which caused me to squint, and couldn't believe the opulence. The floor was the same smooth stone in the slate blue like everywhere else. But that was where the similarities ended. There was a massive claw-foot tub I thought could easily hold me and Theo at the same time. The shower was separate with a glass enclosure. There were double sinks with a marbled stone countertop. I wasn't sure what it was exactly, but it was black with deep gray lines through it. There were sconces on either side of the mirror, which ran the length of the sinks. They were lit from the switch. I learned soon after arriving here to stop trying to figure out how things worked. I chalked it up to magic now.

I stepped farther into the room and noticed my feet were warm. Was the floor heated? Theo could create fire. It wouldn't be a stretch to think he figured out how to heat the stone.

The towels hanging up were big and fluffy. I ran my fingers along the one by the sink. It was so luxurious.

The room was all dark tones, but it worked like everything else here. I didn't think the castle would be the same if it was bright and inviting. It reflected Theo.

I did what I needed to, turned off the light, and went back into the bedroom. I wanted some light to see what was in here. I walked toward the door and found the switch.

It was just like the bathroom. The bed was bigger than a king. I wasn't sure if there was a word for its size, but it must have been custom made. The wood was a deep brown, bordering on black. The headboard was tall with molding creating three different squares on it, all in the same wood. The top of it was flat and created a little ledge. I peered up at it and noticed there were various crystals evenly placed along it. I wondered what they meant.

The footboard was lower and matched the headboard. The nightstands did as well. There were lamps on them with dark shades. The bedding was a rich chocolate. Looking at it now, no wonder I was so comfortable. It was soft and kept me warm. The mattress cradled my body.

In the far corner was a tall armoire. A couple of chairs sat near the windows. They had high backs and didn't look nearly as inviting as the bed. There was a fireplace that wasn't lit.

Rugs were absent here. I had a big one in my room that covered much of the stone floor and gave the room added warmth.

"It was my parents' room." Theo's voice startled me. I

jumped and turned toward him. He was leaning against the doorway with his arms crossed. "When Leven first brought me here, I slept in their bed. I felt closer to them that way. As time went on, I found I couldn't leave. So, Leven helped me update the room a little at a time. Same with the bathroom. Until it was more my taste and less theirs."

"It's beautiful."

"My father had the mattress custom made with the best materials he could buy. Money was never an issue with him. If he or my mother wanted it, he'd buy it." His eyes met mine. "Are you feeling better?"

"I am. Thank you for taking care of me."

He nodded and focused on the bed. I had the sudden sense of loss without him watching me.

The clock on the nightstand read nine thirty. I went over to the windows and opened the long, black curtains. They felt like velvet and were heavy.

Sun didn't pour in. If there was one thing I'd learned living here this past week, it was Theo shrouded any strong light with his magic. We did get day and night. The sun and moon were present though they were muted, never having either at full strength. So, the light came in but not brightly.

I glanced back at Theo over my shoulder. He was still in the doorway but this time he was watching me. He had stubble along his jaw and cheeks that had grown in a little more. His hair was mussed. And his clothes were wrinkled, his pendant absent. He looked tired. Was he awake all night watching me?

I turned away and looked out the window. Just because Theo was in here when I woke didn't mean he spent the night here.

He came over and stood by my side, about an arm's length away. The light brightened him a little more.

Vampires could go out in the sun. They walked beneath the

bright rays. From what I'd learned, it wasn't always that way. Many centuries ago, the sun would burn them, but they evolved. Their skin changed. Now there was nothing left of those other vampires.

Most of the elders had died slowly, leaving the royals I knew of in their stead. Some of the families were ruthless, killing off members so they could succeed and rule the families. That was how they did it. Because vampires were immortal. The only way to get rid of them was to kill them. And many did.

One of the families, the Kades, their ancestor killed his wife. Murdered her in her sleep so he could make his lover his bride. What he didn't expect was his son to exact revenge and kill him the same as he did to his wife.

Battle of the fittest, I guessed. Vampires weren't immune to politics or turmoil. They dealt with things humans did, except they did it with a lot more money and no risk of our government coming down on them. As long as they didn't harm humans, they were left alone.

Decades ago, they tried forming special task forces to police the vampires, but they failed at every turn. The vampires and the government came to the agreement that they would handle their own people. It had worked well since. Or at least from everything I'd heard.

Yet here was Theo, a victim in his family's crime. Not in the same sense as the poor humans who lost their lives. Theo lost everything that day. And has lived with the pain since. Shutting himself in this castle. Afraid of everything beyond these stone walls.

Maybe one day I could convince him to leave. Convince him it wasn't all terrible. But what did I know? The humans, the government, the other royals could reject him and make things worse. I'd have to think more on this.

8

THEO

Sickness wasn't something I was used to dealing with. Leven was always healthy thanks to drinking drops of my blood. It extended his life, but it also kept him in peak health.

The moment I saw Paxton was in pain, everything else faded to the background and my sole focus became him. I didn't know what to do. Migraines were only things I'd read about, never experienced. I remembered medicine. Pain relievers. While Paxton was asleep in my bed, I went searching for them, only to find Leven had stocked a bathroom for him.

And the fact that I put Paxton in my bed, that action didn't go unnoticed. I didn't think at first. Simply scooped him up and put him there. Once he was asleep, with his face scrunched in pain and whimpers leaving his lips every time he rolled over, I couldn't imagine him anywhere else. The beds in the castle were good, although mine was the best.

Once I had the medication, I read the label and took out the appropriate dose. It wasn't like I could wake Paxton and ask him if he wanted some of my blood. That would require a lengthier discussion.

I wracked my brain for anything else that would work,

finally remembering the crystals. Leven kept them in his room and office. Hell, he put them all over the damn castle. He explained them to me. Said he got them from Novus and each crystal had different properties. Some healed. Some cleansed. Others affected energy. The list went on and on. I searched everywhere for the ones I thought would help.

Selenite, amethyst, lapis lazuli, and fluorite. I gathered them and spaced them on top of the headboard of my bed. I didn't know if they would do anything. That was Leven's thing. Never mine. But it was worth a shot.

The first time Paxton woke, I was there. I didn't leave him for long, afraid he might need something. I gave him the medicine and he went back to sleep. The next time, I wasn't in the room, but I wasn't far. I couldn't leave. If I tried to walk farther than down the hall, it was like there was an invisible string pulling me back in Paxton's direction.

His gaze ran over my belongings, the things that had been in my bedroom for quite some time. I simply watched him. He was feeling better and moving around, which made me happy. We talked briefly.

The day had worn on and I'd barely said more than a few words to him. What the hell was the matter with me? I spend the night beside the bed, hoping he would be okay and now I was walking the halls like a lost puppy. The invisible collar would pull every now and then, reminding me I should go back to where Paxton was, but I fought it, didn't want to do that because I didn't know what to say. I was a coward running from a human.

Eventually, I found myself in the library, browsing the spines of paperbacks and hardcover books. The room wasn't tall with multiple levels of books, but it was long. Down on the first floor, on the side of the castle where my bedroom was, this was my favorite room. The smell of the books, the comfortable

The Ostin Heir

chairs and couch, the low light, it was perfect. But even in this room where I'd spent so much of my time, I was still missing the man who resided in the castle with me.

My fingers trailed along one of the shelves when I heard him come in. I pretended at first I didn't, kept walking slowly, touching the spines of the books.

"There you are," he said.

I stopped and turned. "Were you looking for me?"

"I didn't know if there was something you wanted me to do. I've done the laundry. Yours is on your bed. I didn't want to invade your privacy by putting it away. It's not time for dinner yet." He shrugged.

"Paxton, I don't need you to do my laundry for me. I can cook, clean, do everything I need to."

"But if I don't, then you don't really need me here, do you?" He turned away quickly but not before I caught the hurt in his eyes. I wasn't sure what to make of it.

Abandoning my walk around the library, I stepped over to him and used my finger to draw his attention back to me. I had to remind myself to be gentle with my touch and my words. I wanted to tell him I did need him, more than I was willing to admit. Instead, I said, "If I didn't need you, Leven wouldn't have selected you to come here."

"I need a purpose, Theo. I'm not used to sitting around and doing nothing. It's not like there's a TV here or internet. Everything is very…"

"Ancient." I dropped my hand and turned back to where I was before. This whole castle was old and so was I. Granted, vampires lived an infinite number of years. That didn't mean Paxton wanted to be stuck here with me. I didn't want him to leave though.

"Theo."

"You can move your things into any bedroom in the castle

you desire." The words were out before I thought the better of them. Or the meaning behind them. What I wanted to tell him was to move his things right next door to mine, yet I didn't voice that. "The bathroom is still stocked from when Leven did it. Unless you don't want to move." I couldn't meet his eyes. Didn't want to see his rejection of what I was offering.

"Why did you move them to begin with?"

"I told you I was angry."

"You did but that wasn't much of an explanation."

It took everything in me not to turn and tell him it was none of his business why I did it. I bit that back and settled on the truth. If I was hoping for Paxton to stay, I couldn't feed him lies. "Leven was gone. That hurt more than I can explain. Then you were here. A man I'd never met, who I didn't want to know, and after decades I had to let someone new into my life while mourning the loss of a man who was dear to me. I couldn't have you near me, staying in a room that wasn't meant to have anyone in it."

I took a deep breath and let it out before continuing, "Do you know what it's like to depend on someone else for food, supplies, anything that isn't in the one place you feel safe?"

"No, I've never depended on anyone in my life. People have always let me down." He was closer now, no longer near the entrance of the room.

I didn't move from where I stood but didn't turn around to face him either. "I hate it. Hate living like this. Hate that I don't get to live like the other families where they do as they please. I don't want to flaunt my money. I just want to be happy."

"You don't have to stay here. You can take the boat and head to the coast."

I turned around with my fists clenched by my sides. "No."

"You're not your family."

I walked toward him with heavy steps until I shared his breath. "You don't know me."

"I know enough that I can say you'd never deliberately hurt anyone. That you miss being around others. That this isn't a home to you but more like a prison." The words hit the center of my chest with their accuracy.

"There's no guarantee I won't turn into them. Get the same blood craze they had. Feed on humans. Drain them dry."

"I've been living here for a week, and you haven't tried to drink from me. That should tell you something."

"Just because I haven't doesn't mean I don't want to. I've never drank from a human or vampire vein. Never sank my teeth into someone's neck and tasted the nectar they provide. Because no one would want me near them even if I chose to. I'm an Ostin. The only remaining member of the cursed family."

"You're not cursed. Something happened. No one knows what, but do you think your parents would want you to live like this? I read about them while I was in school. Saw pictures of them happy. They weren't always the way they were the night everything happened."

"You're right, they weren't. But something triggered them. What if I go on land, walk among the humans and completely snap, start drinking from them? Kill them?"

"I'll be with you. I'll keep a close watch."

Fuck, I wanted to dip my head and trace my nose over his skin. Inhale his scent deep into my lungs. Touch him. Have his hands on me. This close, it was the purest form of torture not to have him how I wanted him. But I wouldn't do anything like that without his consent. Not after all he'd been through.

I made a move to step away, but Paxton reached out and put his hand on my waist. Just one, lightly holding me there. It might as well have been a ship's anchor for the way my feet felt rooted to the spot.

"You wouldn't be able to stop me," I told him. "If something happened. I'm much stronger than you."

He watched me for a moment. I wished I could read his mind. That was a power my family line didn't have but the Xander family did.

"What was Leven?" he asked, throwing me off. I didn't expect that question.

"He was like a father to me."

"No, not that. What was he? He wasn't a vampire, right?"

"He was a human, who my father hired to assist us. But he soon realized Leven was much more than that. He helped around the house. Would escort my mother when she went shopping if my father was unable to do so. Leven tended to our home. Anything my father needed. He did it all. He was also a seer. A human still but with an ability."

"How did he live so long if he was a human?"

"He drank my blood. Not much. Drops at a time to keep him healthy and alive."

"It only works for so long."

"Yes. Leven knew his time was coming to an end. He was a hundred and twenty-three the day he died."

"Vanished."

I nodded. "The blood changes the makeup of the human. He couldn't die the way humans can. But it doesn't work forever. When their life is up, they disappear. I offered to change him into a vampire. He didn't want that. I was going to…" I couldn't say the rest. Wasn't sure if Paxton wanted to hear it.

"What?" His eyes were pleading with me.

"When you were in pain, I didn't know what to do. I thought about my blood and that it could help, but I didn't want to offer it when you were in that state. Even now I'm not sure it's the right thing to bring up. It could help, though it's not something to choose lightly."

"Thank you for your honesty. I appreciate you telling me."

I nodded. He didn't say yes or no either way, but he also didn't run screaming from the room.

"Do you want to show me your library?" he asked. The way this man changed subjects gave me whiplash. It was also a nice way to get off the heavy topic of my blood and onto something lighter like books.

Books I could talk about. Books I could live in, escape, be someone else.

I loved being able to share this with Paxton.

9

PAXTON

Two days later, I finally decided to move my things to a bedroom closer to Theo. I wasn't sure which room Leven originally had me in, but as I carried an armful of shirts around the castle that was an incomplete circle, I decided I wanted to be next door to Theo. I liked my sea view, even if it was always foggy. I didn't want to look out onto the middle of the island.

The room I chose was to the right of Theo's. The furniture was a washed gray wood. The headboard had wide planks with a simple frame around them. The footboard was low with one plank and the same framing. There were two nightstands and a tall dresser. The bedding was a soft sea green. It was simple and looked comfortable.

I hung the shirts in the closet, still on the hangers from when I took them from the other one, and opened the window to let the salty air in. I wasn't sure what it was about it, but it helped me feel at peace. Always had when I was on Desolate. That didn't change here. If anything, I felt closer, more at home, which was odd considering the circumstances.

Diagonal from the room was the bathroom Theo told me about. I started showering in it after Theo mentioned it. I didn't want to move everything from it unless I was sure I was going to stay on the other side of the castle. Now I was glad I didn't.

Theo was somewhere in the castle. His bedroom door was open, and I couldn't help but peer in when I walked by. It was empty. It wasn't until I was on my second trip with an armful of pants on hangers that I ran into him.

He stopped when he saw me. "You're moving?"

I nodded. "I took a room next to yours. I hope that's okay."

"Yes, of course. I can help." He didn't give me a chance to reply before he was pulling the pants from my arms and going into the bedroom to hang them up. I stood there stunned for a second, then got my ass in gear and went back to my old room for more.

It took a few trips, but Theo and I eventually got everything moved. I was sure to carry my boxer briefs. Theo doing that felt too weird.

With everything finally in its place, I sat down on the bed, noting how soft it was. Not as luxurious as Theo's bed but better than the one I had in my apartment.

Theo was lingering in the doorway, not really in but not out either.

"What do I do about my apartment?" I asked him.

"What do you want to do?"

Theo had been honest with me about some things. Well, I thought he had. I had no way to know for certain. I figured I should be honest too.

"I have to go back to the coast in a few days. Do a supply run." I ducked my head, not wanting to see the look on his face when I said this next part. "I thought about not coming back here. Just taking the boat and staying there." I glanced up partway. Enough to see his fists clench. "I-I don't want to do that. I want to be here with you. If you'll have me that is. I can't replace Leven, but I can try and help. Be here for you." Being vulnerable wasn't something I was good at. It went against everything inside me. Right then, I felt like I was exposing my throat to him.

"I won't force you to stay." His tone was somewhere between anger and hurt.

"I know." I did now. Back when I first got here, I didn't.

"Leven didn't give you the choice. Not like he had."

I shook my head. "I didn't know the man, but from what I've learned, he wouldn't have left a child to fend for himself. Once you got older, yes, he had a choice. He could have left but didn't. And then he took the time to find someone to be here. For you."

"I'm not good at this," he grated out between clenched teeth.

"You think I am?" I laughed humorlessly. "I grew up with no one wanting me. No one giving a shit if I did well in school. They cared if I ate, of course. Because if I got sick or malnourished, the state could've taken me away. I was making that family money. But no one cared about me as a person." I got up and walked over to the open window. Let the air pull into my lungs. This time it didn't calm me like it usually did.

"You socialized. Met other kids. I don't understand every cue. I don't read people well."

"Those kids bullied me, Theo. I was small back then. Old clothes. Never had what was in fashion or whatever the hell you want to call it. Everything about me was a target for their teasing. Now, I'm taller, but still not intimidating. They look at me like prey."

"Like I did when you got here."

I turned to find him leaning his back against the wall by the door. His hands were in his pockets. Bare feet braced, legs straight, and his head was down.

"You didn't expect me," I said. "Plus, you had a loss to deal with. Do I think you handled it well? Hell no. Knowing what I do now, I understand though."

Here was this vampire. This strong man who had more money than I could ever know what to do with. Money that would change things for me back home. Money I was earning by being here though we didn't discuss how much yet. With that money I wouldn't have to fear for my life at night. Or wonder what I was going to eat the next day. However, that money wouldn't solve my loneliness. My lack of friends. Companionship. Someone who gave a shit. Even as an adult I didn't have that.

I thought of Leven. He cared about me in a creepy, stalkerish way, but he did. He saw something in me and knew I'd be the perfect person to come here and stay with Theo. It wasn't just about supply runs. About food and chores. Theo needed more than that. Admitting it was a different story.

That life, the one I abandoned, I didn't want it anymore. I certainly didn't need it if I was here. I could go back, collect my meager belongings, grab the items Theo and I needed and come back here.

I couldn't resist the pull to Theo any longer and went to him. I didn't touch him, couldn't do that yet. It wasn't that I was afraid of him. That initial fear I had when I came here was gone. In its place was uncertainty.

Theo was a lot like Desolate Beach and Sparkling Beach. Both vastly different. Both with their own appeal. Light and dark. Much like the man in front of me. Because that was who he was. A man. Being a vampire was only a piece of him.

"What do I do about my apartment?" I asked the question again. The one I didn't get an answer to.

His head lifted, dark eyes that I now knew weren't solid black. They were a shade or two lighter. Enough that this close I could tell them apart from his pupils. I could so easily get lost in them. He wanted to speak. His mouth opened and closed.

"I want to stay," I confessed. "With you."

The tortured look on his face was almost my undoing. "I could hurt you."

"You won't."

"This life is boring. Living on the island."

I shrugged. "Better than working my ass off to barely survive."

"I can't give you everything you want. All I have is here."

I lifted my hand and cupped his cheek. He didn't pull away. In fact, he leaned into my touch. There were words I wanted to say. Ones that would confess more than I was ready to. It was one thing to let him in piece by piece. Show him I wasn't going to run. That I wanted to be here. It was another to put my heart in my palm and offer it to him.

Did I love him? No. But I cared for him. It was moments like this that made me. When he was trying so hard but didn't always give voice to what he was thinking.

"I can't read you," he said. "You say and do things I don't expect."

"Someone has to keep you on your toes." I smiled shyly.

Then, for the first time in almost two weeks, Theo smiled back. Straight white teeth. A bottom lip I wanted to bite. Fuck, he was handsome.

I almost leaned in and kissed him. Instead, I brought my arms up and looped them around his neck so I could hold on to him. To hug him.

His arms came around me, tight. His nose pressed against my neck. I heard him breathe me in.

Every part of me was aware of every part of him.

When was the last time someone hugged me? I couldn't

remember. How sad was that? The last guy I dated didn't. Hell, we never did more than kiss.

Maybe that was how this was supposed to be. Maybe Theo was the one meant to give me the comfort I craved for so long.

"I'm coming back," I whispered. "You might not believe me, and that's okay. I'll prove it to you."

He shook his head where it rested with his forehead on my shoulder. "Pack your belongings and bring them here."

"Okay." I could do that. Easily. Giving up that apartment would be no hardship. I could do that first. I didn't have much. The clothes here were better. But there were a few things I wanted to bring. Then I could drop the key off with my landlord. I was paid through this month. Afterward, I could get the supplies needed. The food.

Theo held me for a while. Not letting go. Not asking for more. And I was fine with that. Content to be here and be held.

From what I'd gathered, Theo hadn't ever been with anyone. Never had sex.

I wasn't about to strip and offer him my body. More of these hugs? I wanted that. With him. He was the first person I trusted in a long time, and I hardly knew him.

My gut hadn't steered me wrong before. I didn't expect it to now. It told me I could be happy. Safe.

I still had a lot to learn about Theo, about vampires. School had only taught me so much. I wanted him to be happy, not merely exist. I wanted to show him things weren't as scary as they seemed. I wanted to bring him back to life.

Getting him on the boat, back to the coast, wouldn't be easy and I'd never force him. I had a feeling it would be a good thing for him. Sometimes the benefits outweighed the risks.

Everything with Theo was a risk. I accepted that. So far, the benefits were worth it.

10

THEO

Tomorrow Paxton would leave for the mainland with a list of things we needed and a note from Leven with where to purchase them. I believed Paxton when he said he wanted to stay with me. I didn't think I'd breathe a sigh of relief until the trip was done and he was back here though.

The last time someone went to the mainland, he didn't come back.

It had only been two weeks since I'd lost Leven. It felt much longer. While Paxton didn't fill the hole Leven left, he filled a different part of me. One that had been sitting dormant for so long. Awakened by his touch.

We hadn't done more than hug. It sounded so juvenile, yet that bit of comfort was addicting. During the day, Paxton made a point to touch me every now and then. A simple hand on my arm. A palm on my back. And for the past two nights, he hugged me before we went to bed. I wanted to pull him into my room and tuck him into my bed. To hold him while we slept.

It wasn't that I didn't want more. I was turned on every time Paxton was near. I'd mastered the art of making sure my hips didn't meet his while we hugged. If they did, he'd feel my very pronounced dick against him.

I lay in bed now, shirtless and in nothing but boxer briefs, staring up at the dark ceiling, the way I'd been for hours. My mind raced with the things that could go wrong when Paxton left. Scenario after scenario. None of it was good. Leven would tell me not to worry. That it wouldn't get me anywhere. But he wasn't here to remind me of that.

There were times when I caught myself staring at something that brought to the surface a memory of Leven. Brought tears to my eyes. I wished he would have taken me up on the offer to turn him into a vampire. Though if he had, I wouldn't have met Paxton.

I scrubbed a hand over my face.

Paxton.

I didn't know what to do with him. What this was between us. I couldn't understand why he wanted to stay here. He wanted to hug me. To touch me. He didn't fear me or run away when I was near. It made no sense.

Then there was the part of me that ached to drink from him. It wasn't uncontrollable. Not like what my family had. When I held him, in addition to getting hard, my fangs would extend. The need to drink was strong. I never felt like that around Leven. Then again, I wasn't attracted to him.

Leven tried to teach me about vampires. About what he knew, including how part of the connection a vampire had with their love interest was drinking from them. I'd heard stories growing up of vampires falling in love with humans, only to drain the life out of them then mourn the loss. It happened centuries ago and was the reason vampires turned humans into their kind. Well, one of them. Vampires did things they wanted like changing humans so they could expand their family. So, they could have more allies. And on and on.

I couldn't drink from Paxton as he currently was. I wouldn't be able to stop once my teeth sank into his flesh. I had a feeling he'd be delicious. So, I kept those thoughts and my fangs to myself.

The gentle lap of the sea against the stone surrounding the island was soothing. I had my window open, something I never did at night before Paxton showed up. He told me how it calmed him, so I tried it. It didn't have quite the same effect on me. I was no less lulled to sleep than before I had the window open.

A sound drew my gaze to the window. At first, I thought it was the windowpane moving. Then I heard it again. This low, deep noise. I got out of bed and went to the window, opened it more, and listened.

There it was again. This time I knew exactly what it was.

Paxton's room was directly next to mine. And his window was surely open. The walls in the castle were thick. Sound didn't travel through them. Through open windows it would.

The moan was easily recognizable now. It wasn't the kind derived from pain. It was from pleasure.

"Fuck," I whispered as I began to harden, my dick filling the front of my boxer briefs.

I'd never heard that noise from anyone other than myself. If Leven enjoyed his hand, I didn't know about it and was grateful for it.

I leaned forward, trying to listen hard. I shouldn't be doing this. Paxton deserved his privacy. But I was damn horny all the time.

Reaching into my boxers, I pulled my dick out and began to stroke it. Precum pearled on the tip and acted as lube. It felt so good to stroke myself. I wondered if Paxton was doing the same thing. If he was touching himself like I was. Maybe he was fingering his ass. Or maybe he was fucking his fist.

A moan slipped past my lips before I clamped my mouth shut. I hoped he didn't hear me. Chances were he did, given how close to the window I was. If I could hang out and stare into his room, I would at this point. Apparently, I didn't have boundaries anymore.

I wanted to go into his room. I wanted to touch him. Show him he didn't have to do this alone. That I could be there for him. Would he want that with me? He alluded to it before. That might have been in the heat of the moment and didn't mean anything.

While I loved listening to Paxton, I wanted more friction. I wanted the fantasy of him beneath me. I went to the bed and laid down on top of it. Started thrusting my hips against it. My eyes slipped closed, and I pretended it was Paxton I was on top of. That it was his body bringing me pleasure.

I moaned loudly, unable to help myself. The window was still open. Paxton could have heard me. I was too amped up to care.

My ass flexed with every thrust. I used my thighs. It felt good but I wanted more.

A knock on my door paused my movements.

"Theo," Paxton said from the other side with a strained voice.

"Shit," I muttered and quickly pulled my boxer briefs up and tucked my dick back inside. I went over to the door, sure to hide my waist behind it when I opened it.

What I didn't expect was Paxton on the other side stark naked. His dick was hard; his hand fisted around the base.

"Paxton, what are you..." My tongue felt too thick for my mouth. He was gorgeous. Not overly muscular but lean and slightly defined. There was a smattering of hair on his chest. Enough that I wanted to run my fingers through it. Not too much where I couldn't see his nipples, which were pebbled.

"I don't want to be alone. I heard you. Can we... get off together?"

"Together?" To do this with another person, to touch them, come with them, my dick throbbed.

"I don't have to touch you or vice versa but I could hear you, Theo. I'm so fucking turned on. I want to see you too."

Goddamn. How did I resist that?

I pushed my underwear down and stepped out from behind the door, showing myself to Paxton and just how hard I was.

"Jesus, you're huge."

"Am I?" I looked down. I didn't have a point of reference. Except for Paxton and he didn't look much smaller than me. A little thinner maybe. And his had a slight curve.

He nodded. "I wonder if my hand could fit around you."

"Paxton," I warned. The more he talked, the more I wanted to reach forward and pull him into my arms. To feel his body against mine. To taste his lips.

"I won't do anything you don't want me to."

"Don't you realize that you are the one person who could do whatever they wanted to me, and I'd not only allow it, I'd enjoy it, no matter what it was?" I trusted him. More than I probably should.

He stepped into the room, slowly like he was afraid if he moved too fast, I'd run. But that was the furthest thing from my mind. If I was running anywhere, it would be right into his arms.

His dick jerked when he was within touching distance of me. He reached out hesitantly. The first brush of his fingers felt like a live wire was attached to him and sent a jolt of electricity through my body. His next touch was firmer, pressing my dick against my stomach so he could stroke me with the backs of his fingers.

Finally, he wrapped his hand around my length and

stroked. My knees nearly buckled. How could something as simple as his hand on me feel this good?

"You're like velvet-coated steel," he murmured.

I put my hand on his shoulder, unsure if he wanted me to touch him and too cowardly to ask. I'd never do something he didn't want me to and after what he told me about being raped, I didn't want him to think that I was capable of taking something from him he didn't want to give.

"Paxton," I whispered.

His eyes met mine. "Let me take care of you. I want this."

I nodded. My eyes stayed open. I needed to watch him. Needed to etch every part of this in my memory for fear it wouldn't happen again.

He started off stroking me slow until I bucked into his hand, then he picked up the pace. His wrist twisted, changing the sensation. I moaned.

"I can't hold back much longer," I confessed. I was surprised I lasted as long as I had.

"It's okay. Let go, Theo."

He pumped me a few more times before lightning shot through me, and my eyes slammed shut. My free hand reached for his forearm so I could feel more connected to him. His muscles flexed with every movement. My hips bucked, and I came.

Paxton's name tore from my lips. He was relentless, not letting up, kept milking me. My body trembled. I was along for the ride as Paxton worked me over.

Eventually, I couldn't take it any longer and became too sensitive. I stilled his wrist. Looked at him through hooded eyes and dragged my gaze downward to see the evidence of my release painted over his skin. He looked better with me on him.

"Holy shit that was hot," he said then used his hand covered in my cum and wrapped it around his own dick.

Vampires didn't carry diseases. We couldn't pass anything to humans, and they couldn't give us anything. I was sure Paxton knew that, especially when he dragged his other hand through the cum on his stomach, brought it to his lips, and sucked it off. My spent dick twitched at the sight.

I stepped closer so his dick brushed my body when he stroked it. "Come on me, Pax. I want to feel you."

He cried out and started coming. Shots of his hot release landed on my stomach, my dick, and my hip. I wanted to rub it all over my body. To cover myself in him. But refrained. Another thing that might scare him away.

"Fuck," he panted and dropped his forehead to my shoulder. "I don't think I've ever come like that in my life." I knew I hadn't.

We stood there until our breaths slowed. Paxton raised his head and our eyes met. I opened my mouth to talk but he shook his head.

"No," he said. "I don't want you to say it was a mistake."

I gripped his hip to bring our bodies flush. "Nothing about this is a mistake. If anything, I want to do it again. You need sleep though. You have to be alert tomorrow when you head to the mainland."

"You're right. I should get to bed." He turned to leave; however, I didn't let go.

"My bed. With me. If you want."

"I do."

We both went into the bathroom, cleaned off, and crawled into my bed together. I wrapped my arms around him and slept soundly with him there.

11

PAXTON

The ride in the boat was smooth. I didn't have to do much of anything. Theo said it was the pendant I wore around my neck that gave the boat the power to follow the path it was on. Magic. I made sure the pendant was tucked under my shirt. I didn't want someone to pull it from my neck while I was out today, thinking it was something valuable. It was, but not in the way they'd expect.

Leaving the island wasn't easy. Theo didn't say much and neither did I. The weight of what I was doing was there though. I told him I was coming back and meant it. He still worried I wouldn't. He didn't have to voice it for me to know.

I had my own fears about this. Not the shopping and getting things on the list part. The credit card in my name that was in the envelope Leven left me was tucked into my wallet. I still didn't know how he managed that, considering my credit rating had to be shit, and I still didn't talk to Theo about a wage for me. I might never. I was getting free housing and didn't need much of anything except food.

Today, I had to go to my apartment before I ran the other errands. And that scared me more than anything. I knew who would be there at this time of day. Who would torture me, make me fight to get away. Those items inside that tiny space I called home for years, I wanted them. The fight was hopefully going to be worth it.

The boat stopped at the same pier where I met Leven that day. I made sure to tether it and shut off the engine. It wouldn't run without me and the pendant. No one would be able to steal it.

Children playing on the beach drew my gaze to them. They laughed and ran around. Happiness that used to be so foreign to me. Being with Theo last night, I had gotten a taste of it. What it felt like to smile and relax. Damn, if I didn't want much more of that.

No one paid me any attention as I got on the pier and made my way down to the road where I'd last parked my car when I went for a walk on Desolate. I stopped when I got there. It was gone. No doubt towed or stolen. So much for that.

The sun was beating down on me, not too strong yet since it was only May but soon it would be worse. Hot and humid.

I walked to my apartment. Along the way I pulled out my phone and downloaded the app that would allow me to request a car to drive me to the store. Thanks to Leven and his creepiness, there was a phone charger at the castle with a bright pink sticky note beside it saying the bill would be paid monthly and not to worry about it. I didn't want to run from my building on foot. A car would be better. I entered in my information including my new credit card number and ordered the car. Ten minutes until it arrived. I had it stopping a block over from my apartment. I might have to run that one block, but nothing after. Once I was away from here—this shithole I once called home—I wasn't turning back.

From the outside, the building wasn't anything to look at. Peeling white paint over red brick. Windows that didn't open all the way from the hinges being rusted. Railings on the small balconies that looked like they'd collapse if someone leaned on them. There was no one lingering out here. I knew better though. The real danger was inside.

My apartment was on the second floor. When I rented it, I was grateful for that, thinking no one could break in up there. I was wrong because the threat wasn't coming from outside.

Slowly I approached my door, deliberately keeping my steps light, listening for sounds of anyone nearby. The apartment door was intact. No evidence of splintered wood from being broken into. No, they only did that when they knew I was in there.

It was the jingling of the keys that had Chuck's door opening like he was fucking listening for the sound.

"Well, well, well," he sneered. He looked me up and down. Greasy hair fell forward onto his forehead. His clothes looked like they hadn't been washed in weeks. Bile rose in my throat.

I knew better than to wear the nice clothes Leven bought for me. If I showed any inclination that I had somehow gotten money, Chuck would have known and beaten me even harder. As it was, I was pushing my luck.

My mind checked back in, and I rushed to shove the key into the lock, struggling to get the door open. I wasn't fast enough. A fist landed against my right kidney. Pain shot through my body, but I kept trying to get the door open.

A meaty hand gripped the back of my neck as I was pushed against the door. Rancid breath reached my nose. He was too fucking close. I had to get away.

"You know better than to try and run from me, Paxy. I only want what's owed." He ground himself against my ass. There was no missing how hard he was.

I trembled in fear, wanting to go to that place where I didn't feel what was happening. Where I didn't smell him. Couldn't hear him. I couldn't do that this time. Not when Theo was waiting for me, depending on me to get the things he needed.

Bringing my foot up, I slammed my heel back into Chuck's shin. He wailed and released me. It was enough that I could finally get the door open and slam it shut before he was pushing inside with me. I immediately reached for the dresser I kept near the door and slid it over. It would only buy me so much time though. I knew from experience that Chuck didn't mind going into the apartment directly next to mine where one of his asshole friends lived. Where he'd climb over the balcony to get to mine.

I raced around the apartment, grabbed my backpack, and went for the loose floorboard under the shitty area rug I had. Everything inside, I stuffed into my bag as fast as I could, then raced toward the balcony.

The rusted door squeaked as I slid it open. The drop down wasn't terrible. I'd done it before. It would hurt but not as much as Chuck and his friend taking turns raping me.

I straddled the railing and was hoping to slowly lower myself down but that shitty railing decided it had enough and gave way. I fell back, dropping into a heap on the ground. My ankle hurt and so did my side but I didn't waste time to see what the damage was. I heard the other sliding door opening. Heard Chuck shout.

As fast as I could, I ran out of there to the car, which was hopefully waiting for me. I didn't care that I was in pain or that I might have broken something. Nothing mattered except getting the hell away from there.

I rounded the corner and saw the four-door sedan idling. I wrenched open the door and got inside. "Go!" I shouted at the driver.

He turned to look at me then something caught his gaze out the window. Chuck was running toward us.

The Ostin Heir

"Please," I pleaded with him.

The guy put the car in gear and sped off. He could have stayed, let me get pulled from the vehicle. He didn't.

"Thank you," I told him and dropped my head back, not bothering to take my backpack off. So much for leaving my key for the landlord. Whatever. He could take everything in my apartment. I didn't give a fuck. I had what I wanted from there.

"Are you okay?" he asked, his voice shaking a little. "Do you need me to take you to the hospital or anything?"

"No, I just want to get to the store."

"That guy chasing you..."

"Would have beat the shit out of me, among other things, if you hadn't pulled away when you did."

He nodded, keeping his eyes on the road.

The store we were headed to was in the nice part of town where scum like Chuck never ventured. I didn't look like I belonged over there either, but I was going to fake it. This was where Leven said I should go. Where there was a list of things to get and an unlimited budget.

The driver stopped in front of the store. I clicked on the app, made sure to give him five stars, and tipped him generously.

"Thank you," I told him. "You have no idea how much what you did means to me."

He turned. His gentle eyes met mine. "I do. I've been there. Been afraid. I'm glad I could help. Do you want me to wait? I could take you to your next stop."

"Really?" I was prepared to order a different car. I didn't think this guy would want anything else to do with me once he dropped me off.

"Yeah." He gave me a small smile.

"That would be great. Thank you."

I didn't trust the guy enough to leave my backpack in the

car, so I took it with me as I went into the nice grocery store, where everything was so expensive that the price tags almost made me choke. I had to remember this was for Theo. He wasn't about to get a bag of noodles and whatever was on sale that was about to expire.

It was slow going through the store since I was in pain. My back throbbed where I was punched. I was sure I twisted my ankle on the fall. Could have been worse. I got away from Chuck and I never had to see him again.

The driver whose name I never asked for, took me everywhere I needed to go. There used to be a time when these apps gave you information about the drivers. Now it was kept confidential. Too many awful things had happened to them, and they protected their identity. I didn't blame them.

By the time we were back at the pier, I was exhausted from limping around. I had everything I needed and then some. Theo had told me to get whatever I wanted. It felt strange adding things for me that I wasn't paying for, but I reminded myself that I worked for him. Or did I? Theo wasn't someone I looked at like an employer. He was more than that.

Fuck, I didn't know who the hell we were to each other. Last night was amazing. I couldn't believe it happened. And then to sleep with Theo wrapped around me, I felt so safe.

It took a few trips from the car to the boat to load everything. It wasn't just food I had to buy but other supplies as well. Luckily, I was able to find big boxes to haul more to the boat each trip. I didn't want to take too much time and risk the food going bad. The driver offered to help. I asked him to stay by the car and watch the items I bought. We were back in Sparkling Beach where people didn't steal, but I was leery. I wondered if I always would be.

I closed the trunk once I got everything from it and from the inside of the car. "Thank you for everything," I said.

He stuck out his hand. "Zeke. My name is Zeke."

I smiled and shook his hand. "Paxton."

"I'm not sure what you're doing or where you're going, I won't breathe a word of this by the way. Next time you need anything, text me. I'll be here." He handed me a piece of paper with his number on it.

"I will. You helped me out today. I won't forget that."

"I'd like to think someone would do the same for me." He shrugged.

"Until next time." I smiled, not wanting to talk about what the hell I'd been through today, grateful he didn't pry into where I was going on the boat.

He smiled back and waved as I walked away. It was time for me to go home.

Home. Was that what the Isle of Ostin was to me now? I never wanted to set foot in my apartment again. I didn't want to leave Theo, not when I was his only link to the outside world. Theo and I needed to talk.

I sat down in the boat, my side protesting, but my ankle happy to finally have no weight on it. I started the engine, and the boat did what it was supposed to. Took me back to the vampire waiting for me. The one who thought he was cursed.

12

THEO

Here I was again, pacing. Only this time, I started pacing the moment Paxton left. I wasn't going to admit it out loud, but I was nervous and afraid. I didn't think he was coming back. Seeing all that he'd been missing the past two weeks, he could change his mind. I didn't have much to offer him. An old castle. No TV or internet. Nothing but stone, books, the ocean, food, and a vampire who was so afraid he was going to turn into his family that he wouldn't leave the very island he lived on.

Then I heard it. The boat.

I raced down the stairs, through the castle, out the door that took me to the sand. My feet bare, I didn't stop until the ocean lapped at my toes as I watched the boat come in. Relief hit me so suddenly, my shoulders sagged, and my arms went limp. He was back.

Paxton gave me a small smile then turned off the engine.

Every part of me was screaming to go to him. To wrap him in my arms and never let go. While that internal debate was going on, he stood and gingerly stepped out of the boat, a grimace on his face, and secured the vessel.

I was moving before I realized it. "What happened?"

"Nothing. It's fine now." He tried smiling again, only the pain must have made it difficult.

I swept him up into my arms like I did the day he had a migraine.

His hands laced behind my neck to hold on. "Theo, I'm okay."

"If you were then you wouldn't have looked the way you did. You're obviously hurt." Only when we were in my room did I put him down on my bed. "Tell me what happened."

"We have to get the food before it spoils."

"Fuck the food! I want to know why you're in pain."

Paxton didn't flinch at my tone. He looked down at his hands, which were folded on his lap. "I told you I wanted to go to my apartment. Well, my neighbor was there, like always, and he hit me. I fought him off, grabbed my things, and ran. I fell on the way out."

Rage lit my veins. "I'll kill him."

He shook his head. "You won't because he doesn't matter. I'm here now."

I didn't say anything. He was right that I wouldn't hurt him but not because of the reason he said. I'd have to leave the island to kill this man. And to do that I'd have to face my fears. I was a coward plain and simple.

"I'm fine," he said. "Just my side, and my foot hurts a bit. I can still help put things away." He moved to swing his legs off the bed.

"No." I sat down, facing him. "You're not getting up."

"Then go get the food out of the boat. I'm serious about it going to waste."

"If I get it, will you let me tend to you after?"

"Yes, but I don't need you to. I'm capable of taking care of myself."

"I didn't say you weren't. I'd like to help though."

"Fine," he grumbled.

It didn't take me long to get everything off the boat and unpacked inside. There were things I'd never used before. Food Paxton must have gotten for himself. Toiletries. A big tube of lube. That I had used. Far too regularly lately with Paxton living under the same roof. I placed that in his bedside table before I went back into my bedroom.

Paxton was sitting on the bed in the same spot, eyes on me when I entered the room. His feet were bare, sneakers and socks removed. One ankle swollen.

I walked over and sat on the bed again. Gingerly, I took his foot onto my lap. "How bad does it hurt?"

"As long as I don't walk, it's okay."

"I'm going to get you some ice. Take off your shirt while I'm gone so I can look at your side."

"You're very demanding." I swung my gaze his way, thinking he was being serious. He wasn't. He wore a grin. I narrowed my eyes before leaving the room.

In the freezer, I found ice packs Leven had kept there. I grabbed one along with a hand towel and went back to my bedroom.

I froze the second I was through the doorway. Paxton was on the bed, shirtless like I asked. I hadn't prepared myself for the sight of him. I saw him last night like this, but him in my bed without us sleeping was different. My dick took notice. As my eyes raked down his body, I remembered why he was in this position when I saw his ankle. It propelled me forward to place the ice pack wrapped in the towel on his ankle.

"Which side?" I asked him, motioning toward his abdomen.

"Right."

I walked to the other side of the bed and got on my knees by his side. He leaned forward. The area was already bruising. "Pax..." My fingers lightly brushed over the skin. He flinched, making me drop my hand. "I can get another ice pack."

"Sit with me for a bit."

Turning, I did as he asked, brushing my shoulder against his. My fingers itched to touch him. To make sure he was okay everywhere else. How dare someone lay a hand on him. He was here with me. Living in my home. He was *mine*.

"I think we should talk," he said softly.

Was this what I'd read in romances? Where the two people decide what they had wasn't working and stopped everything. We'd hardly started. And here I was thinking we were in some sort of a relationship. Getting possessive over a man, who for all I knew, didn't want me that way again.

I was a fool to think those things. To let myself be vulnerable. This was what happened. I got hurt. I shouldn't be surprised. Paxton was a human and someone who didn't decide this on his own. Yes, he came back, but maybe that was only to stock me up for a bit and leave again.

"Theo."

My name on his lips pulled me from my thoughts. I looked over at him.

"I've said your name three times. What were you thinking?"

I wasn't going to spill everything in my mind. Make myself even more open. "Tell me what you want to discuss."

He sighed. "I thought by me coming back, you'd let down more of your walls."

"What are you talking about?"

"You're guarded. Not that I'd expect differently since you've never…"

"What?"

"You've never been with anyone before, have you?"

I focused on the windows. I didn't want to discuss this, but he deserved an answer after what we shared last night. "No."

"Part of having someone in your life is talking to them. I'm sure you and Leven talked."

"Leven was different."

"I know. So, I'll talk. Just listen and when I'm done you can say anything you want."

I nodded.

"I told you I didn't have an easy past. I've never really done the whole boyfriend thing. I've dated. Nothing serious. But I've also had things happen to me I wouldn't wish on anyone. It's made me be more cautious. I've gotten to know you over the last two weeks. Sometimes it was torture to pull emotion from you—other than anger—but once that first wall cracked, I started to see who you really are.

"The wall I'm talking about is the one you must have built around your heart. I doubt you realized you did so. It probably went up after everything happened with your family and you've been reinforcing it since. It's a safety measure. A way to protect yourself so no one else can hurt you. Leven never would. He proved that. But then he left and there I was.

"When I had the migraine, you opened up more. Last night, again there was this side of you I hadn't seen. I love these glimpses because it shows me who you are. Not this front you put on to protect yourself. If you're wondering how I know about this, it's because I did the same thing. How could I not when time after time people failed me. They kept proving there was no one out there who wanted me."

He was breaking my fucking heart. The one he said had walls built around it. I understood what he was saying. It made sense. That very thing I'd guarded was being shredded with his words. I ached for him. For the boy he used to be who had no one. I might not have had my family but at least I had Leven. I never lacked love.

He continued, "Last night meant something to me. I wasn't

The Ostin Heir

just in here with you to get off, even if I made it seem like that. I wanted that connection with you. To share something intimate. To hear your moans, it was my undoing. Then afterward when you wrapped me in your arms and slept, fuck, I felt cherished. That was a new thing for me. I loved it, Theo. Loved everything we did together. And I want to keep doing it. If you want to as well. But I don't know how to keep my heart out of it. I'm already getting attached to you. To try and keep this just sexual, I'm not sure I can. Do you understand what I'm saying?"

I felt his gaze on me, so I turned to face him. "I understand."

He waited for me to say more. Lifted his eyebrows. "You can talk now."

"Okay. I wasn't sure. I didn't want to interrupt you." Reaching over, I used my pinky finger to toy with his to give me something to focus on while I talked. "I don't know how to have a relationship. My knowledge of them only extends as far as what I saw within my family when I was younger and from what I've read in books. Fiction as they are, there is some truth to them. Romance exists, even if I've never experienced it on that level. I worried while you were gone today. Afraid you'd see what you were missing and not come back. The relief I felt when you did was immense. Then to see that you were hurt, I couldn't be there to protect you. To keep you safe."

I shook my head. "I'm a fucking vampire. Someone who's strong and could have crushed whoever hurt you, yet I was useless. Behind these walls, scared to leave. What do I have to offer you? There's nothing here but me. I have no experience. I haven't traveled. I'm not well spoken. Yet I find myself wanting you. I shouldn't. I'm worried I'm going to hurt you."

"We've been through this," he said. "You won't."

"The blood craze..."

"In seventy years, you haven't had it happen."

"And everything else I said?"

"I don't need more than you. You've heard about my past, my job, where I lived. I gave it up without a second thought. I had nothing there to lose but here, here I have everything to gain." He reached over and put his hand over my heart. "There's a connection between us. I want to explore that. I want to be with you as more than whatever the hell I was when I got here."

"I don't want you to work for me, Paxton." Why was it so hard to tell him I wanted the same thing as him?

"I'm not going to hurt you," he whispered. How did he know what I was thinking?

"I want to try. I'll probably fail, make you hate me, but I can't turn you away. Not after what we've shared."

"Are you sure it's me you want? You could go to the coast and find others to fall for you. There's a whole legion of people who would love to be with a royal vampire."

"Even if you were standing in a sea of people, I would only have eyes for you." Then I leaned forward and kissed him.

13

PAXTON

Kissing Theo was like savoring my favorite flavor of ice cream. Slow and sweet. A hesitant lick here. A slight nibble there.

He didn't dive in and try to consume me. He didn't need to. What he was doing was perfect.

I let him lead, not wanting to push him farther than he wanted to go. This was new to him. Sure, we got off together last night. That was jumping in with both feet. This was the opposite, and I was grateful for it. Theo deserved to be savored. Hell, so did I.

Theo moaned when I reached around the back of his neck, up into his hair and tugged. I wanted to hold him where he was. To let this go on forever. No one had kissed me like this before.

I moved so I could get closer but that made me gasp in a breath when I twisted, and pain shot along my side and into my back.

"Shit," Theo said as he pulled back. "I didn't mean to hurt you."

"You didn't. I moved." I settled back against the headboard and closed my eyes.

"I brought it up before, but we didn't talk about it. I could give you some of my blood to help you heal. The pain would go away. The bruise would disappear, and your ankle wouldn't be swollen anymore."

I peered over at him. Saw the tightness of his features as his eyes focused on my ankle. He didn't need to say anything else for me to understand he felt guilty about what happened to me. He shouldn't have. It wasn't his fault. But in his eyes, I went to the coast for him. He couldn't protect me because he didn't leave the island. Theo had trouble reading me. I was coming to understand him.

"If I drank it," I started, "then I'd have to keep drinking it, right?"

"It would extend your life. Keep you healthy. Alive. If you stopped drinking it, then you'd go back to the way you were. Susceptible to injury, illness, and the like."

"And if I wanted to become a vampire?"

"Paxton..."

"I'm not saying that's where I'm at. I'm curious. Would you change me, Theo?"

His tortured eyes met mine. "If you wanted that, I would. You'd have to be sure. It's not a decision to make lightly."

"You wouldn't need to buy blood anymore. You could drink from me." That wouldn't be why I'd want to become a vampire. I'd finally be strong for once in my life. I wouldn't get bullied, assaulted, raped. I could fight better. I never could afford lessons for self-defense or anything else that could help me. I learned on the fly by doing what I could. I'd been weak for so long. The thought of being more was appealing.

The picture in my head of Theo drinking from me, that had my dick taking notice. What would it feel like? Would it be pleasurable? I'd read it was an experience, but it was different for everyone. It also depended on the relationship between the vampire and the one they were drinking from.

Theo focused on my neck for a moment. His voice shook a little. "You'd let me do that?"

"I told you I trust you. I meant it."

"I never thought anyone would want that from me, considering my past."

"It's your family's past too. You didn't do anything wrong that day. I think the only way you'll get past that, to fully believe in yourself, is to move outside of your comfort zone."

"I'm not ready to leave the island."

"I know. One thing at a time. First, can you open the window for me? I'd really like to hear the ocean."

He got up and went over to it. Both windows opened to let the sound in I loved so much. I moved down to lie on the bed. Theo joined me, lying on his side facing me.

"Why do you like the sound of the water?" he asked.

I reached over to the nightstand where my phone was and pulled up the photos. I found one of Desolate and showed it to Theo.

"Is this where I used to live?"

I nodded. "The whole place was burned to the ground after everything happened. All that's left are shells of the buildings that once stood." I showed him more pictures. Not just of the town but of the beach, the ocean, the fog which I now knew came from Theo, from this island. It surrounded him.

He sat still, except for his finger moving over the phone screen to look at the land. "Why do you have so many pictures of it?"

"I like going there. It's quiet. Not many people. Most stay away from it, instead going to the neighboring beach. We call where you used to live Desolate Beach now and the one just to the north is Sparkling Beach. They're so different." I took the phone and found a picture of them, of that dividing line where things went from dark to light.

"Holy shit," he muttered. "I can't believe it looks like this. Leven told me what they were renamed to, but I'd never seen what they looked like."

"The fog seems to stay right where Desolate is."

"I wanted to keep the island as cloaked as possible. I know it's done so by a mage but anything else I can add to it, I do."

"It makes sense."

"And you prefer to be there, on Desolate Beach?"

"Is that so hard to imagine?" Others couldn't believe it. The few who I talked to on occasion. Not friends but co-workers I'd see.

He handed my phone back. "When I look at it, it still reminds me of the place I used to call home, but it also has the terrors of that night there."

"You didn't ask Leven about it?"

"No." He shook his head. "I said I didn't want to know. The guilt claws at my insides." He reached up and gripped the front of his shirt in a fist. "I used to wonder if I'd ever be rid of it, then I saw it as my penance. No, I didn't kill anyone, but I still was there. It was my family."

"Theo, maybe the first step here is accepting that it wasn't your fault. You were ten years old. A child. There was nothing you could have done."

"I don't know if I can." Okay, this wasn't working. I had to try something else.

"What would you say if I told you it was my fault those men raped me? That my neighbor beat me because I deserved it?"

"No, absolutely not. They shouldn't have done those things to you. They should be dead for committing those crimes."

"But what if I thought I could have done something different? Talked to them to get them to understand what they were doing was wrong?"

"I don't think they would have listened."

I raised my eyebrows, hoping he was catching on to what I was doing here. I wasn't a psychologist, nor had I seen one in my life, but something had to get into Theo's head that what happened all those years ago wasn't his fault. He was a victim too. He lost his family. The people he thought would always keep him safe.

He swallowed. I watched the way his throat worked.

"Do you understand what I'm saying?" I asked.

"Yes."

"It won't be easy to let this go, but I think it will help bring you a measure of peace. You've been torturing yourself for so long. It's time you stopped."

I took his hand in mine and brought it up to my neck, so his fingers pressed to my pulse point. He was riveted to the spot, breathing shallow, completely focused.

"I trust you," I repeated. I'd say it however many times I had to until he understood that he wasn't going to hurt me. That he wouldn't kill me.

His lips parted and his fangs descended. I fought not to flinch away. It was a stark reminder of what Theo was. Sometimes I easily forgot. I saw him as a man and nothing else. But he wasn't. Nor would he ever be. Theo was a vampire and there was no changing that.

"You're so tempting," he whispered as his thumb gently rubbed over my skin.

I tilted my head to the side, exposing more of myself to him. "I like it when you touch me."

"But those men who hurt you—"

"Aren't you. I struggled a lot to be able to welcome someone else's touch again. It wasn't easy, but I worked on it and eventually wasn't afraid when the man I briefly dated did kiss me. You don't try to control me, Theo. Or grip my neck hard. You don't put bruises on my skin or say awful things to me."

"I couldn't. The mere thought of someone doing that to you has my heart racing and my blood pumping, wanting revenge."

This man, this vampire, how could I not trust him? Even with his fangs out and his eyes on the vein in my neck, he didn't make a move. The thing I had to work on was getting him to trust himself. I wanted to take him to Desolate Beach. I wanted him to see what I did when I went there. While a horrible tragedy occurred there, that wasn't all it was. The town could be built anew. The only reason it sat as it did was as a reminder to vampires. Not as a shrine to those who were killed.

Desolate had once been his home. Theo needed to be able to put that part of his life in the past and not live with the reminder of what happened.

I moved on the bed and pain shot through me again. Theo was there, sliding his hand from my neck down my body, soothing me. He probably didn't realize he was doing it.

If I was going to be this person Theo could trust, someone who would hopefully lead him back to a full life, then I had to stick around for a while and I didn't mean a few months. I had to be here for him. Show him I was the one he could rely on. And to do that, I had to make sure I wasn't getting injured every time I was back on the coast. I needed to return to him healthy and not have him worry.

"I want to drink your blood," I told him. I wasn't going anywhere. I was in this with him. How could I leave when he'd shown me so much of himself? I was only scratching the surface. The emotion running through Theo went as deep as the ocean outside.

"You hardly know me. What if you change your mind?

What if you want to leave? You won't stay healthy and strong without my blood. You won't live longer."

"I'm much younger than you, but that doesn't mean I haven't lived a life before I came here. I've been through things most don't experience in their nightmares. Being here beside you feels right. This is where I'm meant to be. I can't predict what will happen in the future. I wish I could, but once I make a decision, I stick to it. I want you to heal me, Theo."

He nodded. Brought his wrist up to his lips. Those fangs of his, one sliced into his wrist. He turned it toward me so I could see the shallow cut. Held it right in front of my lips. "Lick."

I didn't hesitate to lean toward him with my tongue out. I expected the metallic taste of blood flooding my mouth. Instead, it tasted a lot like cinnamon. I swept my tongue over his skin again. His eyes drifted closed, and a low moan left him. I wanted him to do that over and over, so I licked some more. This time he pulled back after. The wound knitted closed before my eyes.

"You taste like cinnamon," I whispered.

"I can make it so my blood is appealing to you. I didn't know if you had a preference. I'd seen you eat a variety of things. So, I went with cinnamon. I'm glad it worked."

"How often do I drink from you?"

"Once a week."

"Always make it taste like cinnamon."

14

THEO

A month had gone by since I first started giving Paxton my blood. I thought it would change things between us. That he would see me as more of a monster than a man. Luckily, it didn't. If anything, it brought us closer.

We spent some nights together in my bed. Others we were apart. We hadn't done anything other than kiss. I didn't want to push Paxton into doing anything he wasn't ready to do. Being with me was a lot.

Paxton assured me he wanted to be here. Yet I worried this was all we were ever going to be. Kissing. Smiling. Sharing meals. Occasionally sharing a bed where I'd get to hold him all night.

After Paxton drank from me, I asked what was so important he had to go back to his apartment. He told me to grab his backpack and showed me the things inside. It wasn't that they were valuable in terms of money. They were items that meant something to him personally.

A stuffed leopard he had found abandoned on the street when he was walking to one of the foster homes. It was dirty and obviously wasn't destined for anything but the garbage. He was only eight or so. He swept it up and brought it home with him, cleaned it off the best he could. At night he said he would pretend it was a pet since that was something he never had.

There was a small yo-yo. It was a cheap toy that was in this prize bin at his school. If a child did really well in class, they got to pick from it. He said most of the kids thought it was all junk, but the few times he had a turn choosing, he cherished those things.

He had a picture of his parents, awful as they were. But it was proof of where he came from, and he wanted that. He also kept his documents like his birth certificate, high school diploma, and anything else he might need.

There was relief on his face that he got to retrieve those items. To bring them to where he lived now. I wished he didn't have to go through what he did to get them. I should have helped but I didn't. I couldn't leave.

Paxton just arrived back from the mainland after another supply run, the boat full of things we needed. Well, not all were needed but most were. Paxton was trying to get me to indulge a little by buying things he thought I'd like. That I needed to try, or so he said. Some of it was food. Some was new soap he said would smell good on me. A few more modern things like a fancier razor for my face. Nothing overly expensive or indulgent. That wasn't Paxton.

Leven had set up a post office box years ago, where he had things shipped he couldn't find in town. He had Paxton's name added as an owner before he died. When Paxton was on the mainland two weeks ago, he ordered items for us. Ones he wouldn't tell me what they were. Only that I would be surprised. I didn't like surprises. I liked knowing what I was getting myself into at all times. I liked to be prepared. That wasn't the case where Paxton was concerned.

Paxton sat next to me at dinner with a mischievous look on

his face. He said nothing happened on the trip today, which I did worry about after he was hurt during his first supply run. But he was different tonight. I couldn't figure out why.

"What?" I asked.

"Nothing."

"This is about the surprise, isn't it?"

"Maybe."

"When do I get to find out what it is?"

"After dinner is cleaned up."

I ate quickly, not giving a shit how I looked. I was tired of waiting to discover what he was up to. I needed to know. My nerves were getting the best of me, and my mind was conjuring up images. I couldn't stand it any longer. I didn't even get a peek in the boat when he came home. He wouldn't let me, so I didn't have a clue what was in there.

He was leaning against the counter when I put the last plate away. "Are you ready?" he asked.

"If you don't show me whatever the hell it is, I swear I'm going to start ripping this place apart."

There was a big smile on his face. My moods didn't affect him. Paxton was numb to them by now. And he was smiling more. So much it made me happy seeing him like that. How I went from being a miserable son of a bitch most of the time to falling in... No. I couldn't go there. Because as much as I loved having him here, I was waiting for it to fall apart. I didn't have anything good in my life except him.

He held his hand out for mine. "Come on."

I took it. Savored the warmth of it against mine. Couldn't believe how long I'd gone without this in my life. Without *him*. Now I'd do anything to keep him with me.

Up the stairs, in my bedroom, he asked me to sit on the bed and wait. I did. It was less than a minute before he was back with a medium-sized box in his hands.

"In here are a few things I bought for us to use. Or you. Depending on how you take them." He stood there, worrying his bottom lip, a nervous habit he had.

"Okay."

He put the box on the floor and pulled out a smaller, long box. "Before I show this to you, I need to ask you something. I probably should have done so before I ordered these, but I figured if you don't like them, I'll keep them for myself." He took a breath and let it out. "Do you want me, Theo?"

I sat, simply watching him, wondering what the hell kind of question that was. "Had I not made that clear?" Maybe I hadn't. I liked him in my arms, in my bed, with his lips on mine. I liked that one time we got off together.

"I'm not doing this right," he muttered then straightened his spine. "I like what we do together and want more. If you do too." He shook his head. "This is ridiculous. I want you, Theo. Really want you. I want to feel what it's like to sink into your body. I want you inside mine. I want it all, with you."

"Are you serious?" No one had ever wanted me like that, not that I'd had the chance to find someone. Yes, Paxton and I spent a lot of time together. He lived here for fuck's sake. He said he wanted a relationship with me, but that didn't mean he wanted me inside him. For us to take this thing between us further. Or maybe it did, and I was just a naïve asshole because I'd never done this before

He nodded. "Very."

I stood, hating the distance that was between us even if it wasn't much. I reached for him, wrapped my fingers around the back of his neck, while my thumb stroked over his skin. "I want that. What you said. I can't promise I'll be any good at it. In fact, I know I won't be. I don't have practice. Don't know what the hell I'm doing."

"That's why I bought this." He handed me the box. I had to release him to open it.

It was nondescript. Lilac in color. There was tissue paper inside slightly darker than the box. Nestled in that was a big fucking cock. Made out of silicone. It was wrapped in plastic and was a bright green color.

I looked up. "It's green."

"Yeah. I thought since you're a vampire and this castle is full of more muted, dark colors, that we could inject some other shades in here."

"In the form of a dildo?"

"You know what it is." He grinned.

"I've lived in this castle for the past seventy years, but I wasn't completely cut off from the world. Leven made sure I had the newest books to read. Kept me up to date on things."

"You talked about sticking things up your ass with Leven?"

"Fuck no! But I know what this is." I took the dildo from the box and held it up. It was heavy in my hand. The thought of putting it in my ass was at the forefront of my mind.

Paxton laid a gentle hand on my arm. "I know you haven't been with anyone before me. I wasn't sure what you've done by yourself. I didn't see any toys in here or in any of the other rooms. Not that I was snooping," he hurried to say. "I've been in here often enough that I've seen you reach into the drawers. Nothing caught my eye. I want to show you how good this can be."

I deflated, the anger leaving me. "I'm sorry."

"You don't have to be. Now put that down and let me show you what else I have in here."

In the box were butt plugs of various sizes, one of them vibrated, and what he called a sleeve that would slide over my dick. Or his. Whoever decided to use it.

The Ostin Heir

Once we went through the items in the box, he set it aside and put his arms around me, his fingers meeting at the back of my neck. "Whether we use these toys or not, I still want you. I just thought this might be a better way to ease you into wanting to be with me. Plus, it's not like we have a lot of entertainment here. I love your library, but I want to do something other than read, eat, and sleep."

I dropped my gaze to the small space between us. "I'm sorry I can't offer you more. This place, it's all I have. There's nothing here. You're young. I understand if you want to leave more often, do other things."

He ducked so he was in my line of sight. "Have you not been listening to me? I didn't say I want to leave. I said I want to be with you. I know who you are and how you live. I don't want to leave and find other things. I just want you. If you don't like what I bought, then throw them out. I don't care. All I want is you, Theo. And if you want to keep things between us the way they are, I'm fine with that too. I didn't mean to upset you."

"I'm sorry." I leaned forward, dropping my forehead against his. It felt like all I did was apologize. "I don't know how to do this. Be that person to you."

"The thing is, you don't have to do anything. I'm happy."

"I want more, like you said. You have no idea how many nights I've lain in bed and thought of what it would be like to be naked with you again. To feel your hands on me and mine on you. To do the things I've only read about."

"Can I take your clothes off, Theo?"

I swallowed and nodded.

Paxton worked his hands under my shirt, slowly lifting it until it was off me and thrown to the floor. He dropped to his knees, a sight I wondered if I'd get to witness. His fingers worked my jeans open and pulled them down and off. He nuzzled his face against my clothed groin. I bit back a groan and resisted plunging my fingers into his hair. He'd gotten it cut while he was away today. It still had a wave to it, but it was shorter, no longer hanging down onto his face, only over his forehead. And lucky for me, he knew how to cut mine. Something he picked up after figuring out how to do it on himself when money was tight.

"You smell so good, Theo." He dragged his nose over my length, which was now hard and aching for his touch.

His hand skated up my thigh until he reached the waistband and inched it down and off. My dick sprang free, bobbing between us.

Paxton looked up at me. "Can I touch you?"

"Anything. You don't have to ask."

I thought he was going to wrap his hand around me like he'd done the other time but instead, he licked my length from root to tip. I bucked forward, pressing against him, unable to help myself. His tongue swept over the tip. This time I didn't hold back and brought my hand to his head, pushed my fingers into his soft hair.

He licked me again, nuzzled some more before he stood and started taking off his clothes. He got his shirt off before I stopped him.

"I want to," I told him.

My fingers moved over his chest and stomach, trailing down until I got to the top of his shorts. There were all kinds in his closet, but I noticed he liked to be more comfortable and chose the cotton ones or the ones that were a lighter material he just had to pull on. Which was what he had on now. No button or zipper to get in my way. Only elastic.

I hooked my thumbs in the waistband and made sure to catch his boxer briefs with it. I pushed them down until I had to crouch to get them the rest of the way off. His dick was there in

The Ostin Heir

front of my face, long and hard. I wanted to taste him like he did me, but was nervous I wouldn't make him feel good, so I stood and wrapped my arms around him, pulling him close.

How did I end up here? This lucky to have Paxton in my life?

15

PAXTON

Buying the sex toys was a gamble. Theo could have seen them and told me to go to hell. But he didn't. I was grateful because now I got to have him like this. It wasn't that I didn't love what we were doing already. I did. His gentle touches. How he cared for me. Kissed me. Held me.

My balls however were hurting, and my hand no longer satisfied me. I wanted Theo with every fiber of my being.

The past month helped me relax more with him. I would have spent every night in his bed if I didn't need time to myself to process everything. I never got a chance to work through the trauma of my past with anyone professional, so I had to do an internal check of myself. Had to be certain this was what I wanted and was ready for.

Theo proved time and again he wouldn't harm me. I was still drinking his blood. Had his vitality flowing through me, keeping me healthy. I didn't feel different outside of the fact that I drank vampire blood. And that didn't freak me out as much as I thought it would.

He started thrusting against me. I reached around and took his ass into my palms, loving the way the muscles flexed each time he moved. Theo was gorgeous and it was in a way that he didn't realize. He didn't care about his looks, outside of making sure he was clean, his hair was cut, and he shaved every now and then.

I wasn't nervous being here, being touched by him. There was no fight or flight instinct. Nothing to tell me I needed to put the brakes on. Because it was Theo and he felt right.

"Do you want to lie on the bed?" I asked. This role of being the leader was new for me. No one normally gave a shit what I wanted or thought. Except for the one guy I dated. No, I wasn't picturing anyone else except the man in front of me. Besides, no one could hold a candle to Theo.

He nodded. "Bring the dildo."

I grabbed it from the box and moved to the bed to lie down next to him. I had already cleaned all the toys before putting them back in their boxes before dinner. Theo wanted to cook tonight so I took the opportunity to get things ready.

There was a tube of lube on the bed between us. He must have taken it from the drawer.

"Whatever you want to do, I'm okay with," I told him.

"Will you use that on me?" He nodded toward the dildo. I knew what it took for him to ask me that.

Theo wasn't a man who liked to be uncertain. He liked to be in charge. Be the one who knew how to handle everything. Since I arrived here, I flipped his world upside down. I watched him change in a good way. Open up to me. Show me there was much more to him than what was on the surface.

Those walls he had around his heart were almost completely down. It took time and a shit ton of trust, but I was getting there, seeing more of him every day. And this, tonight, was a gift I wouldn't take for granted. The fact he wanted me to play with him made me light up inside.

I didn't care if Theo wanted to be the one fucking me. I

never had a preference though others liked to force it on me, taking the choice away. Theo never did. No matter how his moods swung, how irritated he got over a situation, he didn't take it out on me. Didn't touch me in anger.

"Roll to your stomach and spread your legs," I said. He did without reservation. "You've never had anything inside you, right?"

He shook his head.

"I'm going to go slow. I don't want this to be painful for you."

His voice was hard when he spoke next. "I can take it."

I smoothed my hand down his back. "This isn't about what you can handle. It's about what I'm willing to do to you and I'm not going to hurt you."

Moving on the bed, I brought the lube and dildo with me. I settled between his spread legs and dropped some lube on my fingers, rubbing them together to warm it up. I parted his cheeks. His hole contracted right away.

"Shhh," I soothed and reached out to slowly drag my fingers through his crease.

He tensed but I kept going. I rubbed my fingers up and down, not stopping to try and press in yet. Once he relaxed, I brought one finger down and circled his hole, watching as it contracted and released. I dipped my finger in to the first knuckle and stopped. Held it there and waited while I ran my other hand over his ass cheek, loving the tiny hairs there that were soft under my palm.

Theo's face was buried in a pillow he had wrapped in his arms.

"Are you okay?"

"Yes," came a muffled reply.

"You can tell me to stop at any time and I will."

He nodded.

I pulled my finger back, not all the way out, before working it in again, this time to the second knuckle. I gave short thrusts with it, testing to see how he'd react. Having never had anything there, I didn't want this to be a bad experience for him.

When I first did it to myself, I used more lube than was necessary and made a huge mess. I didn't stop until I had two fingers buried inside as I searched out my prostate. It took a few tries before I found it.

My finger finally dipped all the way into him. I stroked around inside, not looking for that magic spot yet, just getting him used to me being in there. His body was tense, but I didn't stop. Not unless he told me to.

Taking my time, I worked a second finger in, then a third. I stretched him for a bit, wanting him ready to take the dildo. I pulled out and thrust two fingers back in, crooking them just right until I felt the spot that made his body tense in a different way and he moaned so long and loud it made me grin.

My own dick begged for attention. I left it alone, wanting to focus solely on the beautiful man before me, who the more I stroked inside, the more his hips thrust forward onto the bed.

"Ready for more?"

"Yes, please," he begged. It was a sweet sound. One I wanted to soak in and never forget.

I reached for the dildo and coated it in a healthy dose of lube. This was bigger than my fingers. The one I bought wasn't too large. I wanted to give Theo pleasure, not make him never want to try this again. With any luck, I got to do this repeatedly, and one day, it would be me inside him, not this.

"This is going to burn," I told him. "I promise to go slow."

"Paxton," he pleaded.

I chuckled and pressed the tip of the dildo to his hole. I nudged it, held it there, nudged it a little more. The head slipped in. I didn't push further. Simply waited like I did with my fingers. Then I pushed a little more in, gave it short thrusts, added more lube around his rim. Theo didn't complain but he did tense. I only pressed forward more when his body relaxed.

Once it was all the way inside, I swore we both sighed. Me at the sight of his hole swallowing that green dick up so well. Him at the sensation.

"How does that feel?" I asked, needing to know before I started to move it in earnest.

"Full. I feel so fucking full."

I hummed. "You look beautiful, Theo."

He turned his head to look at me. His hair was mussed, and his eyes half lidded. "I do?"

"You're gorgeous."

"I want you in me, Pax."

"I will be, just not tonight. This is for you." And for me too, but I kept that to myself.

I started a torturous push and pull with the dildo. Fucking Theo at different angles. I did my best to make him feel good, which he did, given how he kept thrusting against the bed.

"Lift up," I told him. I needed my hand on him. He did as I said.

I still had some lube on my hand and used that in time with the dildo to jerk him as I fucked him. It was a matter of seconds before he was crying out until his voice was raw as he shot hot cum all over the bed. His legs trembled as I kept a relentless pace until I couldn't milk anything else from him.

Slowly, I brought him down until I released his spent dick and carefully withdrew the dildo from his ass. He collapsed on the bed, his back moving up and down with every breath.

I dropped the dildo to the side and crawled over until I was lying next to him. I brushed my fingers through his hair, enjoying that I got to touch him the way I did tonight.

"How are you feeling?"

"That was..." he breathed out. "I don't have words."

"Then I did a good job."

He lifted his head and those dark eyes of his looked at me with something I wasn't sure I was ready to put a name to. Something that scared me as much as thrilled me. "Thank you for everything, Paxton. I don't just mean this, but the way you've been. Patient. Understanding. Perfect."

"I'm far from that."

"Let me be the judge of that."

He leaned forward and kissed me. I moaned, still horny as hell, not finding my release yet.

Theo didn't break the kiss as he reached between us and took my dick into his hand. His palm was rough, but I was too far gone to care. This wouldn't last long.

His tongue fucked into my mouth. His hand jacked me. Every part of my body was like one raw nerve that Theo stroked.

Two more pumps of his hand and I was coming in long, hot jets. My eyes were closed as I let the orgasm wash over me. I didn't expect him to get me off, but I was thankful he did. His hand on me was better than mine any day.

His hand slowed while the last of the tremors shook through me. "Goddamn," he whispered.

I opened my eyes and found his on my spent dick. His hand was covered in my cum as was the bed between us.

"Let me clean us up," I told him, but his voice stopped me.

"No. I want to try something."

Theo brought his hand up. Cum covered him like he caught some of it on his palm, instead of letting it all go on the bed. He looked at his fingers for a second before bringing one to his lips and sucking the tip.

"Holy shit," I muttered. Hot didn't begin to describe the scene in front of me.

"I never wanted to taste mine, but yours is more appealing."

"And?" It was his first taste of cum. I had to ask.

"I want to suck you next time."

I wanted to nod and tell him he could do that any time he wanted. If I came off overeager, I was afraid I might scare him away. Instead, I said, "Okay."

After that, we both got cleaned up in the shower. Together. We didn't get off again, though Theo did pay special attention to every part of my body, thoroughly cleaning me. I did the same to him. In some ways it was as intimate as what we just did on the bed.

We were drying off in the bathroom when he asked, "Are you mine, Paxton?"

"Yes," I answered without reservation. He needed that reassurance, and I was more than happy to give it to him, no matter how many times he asked.

"Good, because I've considered you so for quite some time."

I smiled. "Thanks for clueing me in."

He shrugged, draped his towel over the hook on the back of the bathroom door, and took me into his arms again. This was perfect.

16

THEO

The boat rocked gently on the water where it sat in the center of the island, tethered so it wouldn't drift back out. It was a simple thing. Wood. An engine. Components needed for navigation. A propeller. And I was staring at it like it was about to jump out of the water and take a chunk out of my leg.

"We don't have to do this," Paxton said from my right.

Two days ago, he brought up the idea of taking the boat around the island. Not to the mainland. Not to anywhere there were people. Just for a ride on the Atlantic.

Except I hadn't stepped foot off this island in seventy years. That boat was torture and freedom wrapped in one. I wanted the freedom. Desired it on a visceral level. But with that freedom came the torture of actually leaving. I'd holed myself up here for so long I didn't know how to do anything else.

"We won't go anywhere you don't want to," he reminded me. "You can cloak us in all the darkness you want so no one sees us. The boat has a light that will allow us to see in front of it and with one word, the boat will bring us back home."

Paxton found a book in the library that spoke about the boat. It was a manual with notes written inside, thanks to

Leven. How to use the magical aspect of it should Paxton want to. The boat was spelled by Novus and commands were given to it from Leven. As it was, the boat went to the mainland and back. No direction needed. It did more though.

Yesterday, Paxton took it out to make sure he could get it to do what he wanted without me in it. I was nervous because it was Paxton, and I was afraid the boat was going to do something it shouldn't, and he would die. Yes, everything went back to death with me. That was what happened when everyone I loved died.

What this boiled down to was me trusting Paxton. I did. Didn't mean I wasn't petrified to step aboard that boat though.

I felt Paxton's hand take mine. He gave me a squeeze. "One lap," he said. "If you want to come back, we will. If you want to stay out there, we can. You're the one leading this."

I didn't take my eyes off the boat when I nodded. Paxton tugged me forward, not too hard or fast. Enough to get my feet moving one in front of the other.

The center of the island had the sand there but there was a steep drop off in the water. Without it, the boat would have gotten stuck on the land. There was a little walkway from the sand to the boat. Enough where I could step from sand to wood to boat. I stopped on the wooden planks.

Paxton let go of my hand. I wanted to grab it back but refrained. Coming off needy and desperate wasn't how I wanted this to go, even if I was both of those things.

He dropped down onto the boat then held out his hand for me to take. I looked at it. Moved my gaze to the man who was quickly capturing my heart. His eyes were soft, holding mine in a way that begged me to trust him. To reach out and let him lead. I inhaled a long breath and did just that. My palm touched his again. I walked forward and held my breath as I stepped onto the boat. It rocked beneath my feet.

The Ostin Heir

"You did good," he said and kissed me. "I'm proud of you."

I scoffed. "I got on a boat, not the mainland."

"Don't discount what you're doing. This is a huge step." I felt ridiculous making such a big deal of this. Paxton's praise I welcomed, even if I didn't deserve it.

He led me over to the seats and we both sank into them. Paxton gave me the time I needed to adjust. This wasn't the same boat Leven had brought me here on all those years ago. This was the third boat since then. Leven liked to keep up with technology and wanted us to have the best. I didn't care what he spent. He would never empty me out and it wasn't like I had a lot to spend money on.

"Are you ready?" Paxton asked.

"No."

"We can go back inside. I told you I'd take this however slow you wanted."

"If we get out of this boat, I'm not sure I'll ever get back in it. Just do it. Get us out on the ocean and back so I can breathe again," I whispered.

He leaned over and kissed me once more. The engine started. Paxton said something to the boat that allowed him to take full control of the operation of it.

"I've never actually driven a boat before yesterday," he told me as he started to maneuver us around and toward the narrow path that would lead us out. "Before I came here, I'd never been on one. I'm sure I keep getting the terminology wrong. The manual told me how to use this boat, and luckily there was another book in the library with more details. It's a good thing Leven had a boating license made for me so if the Coast Guard stops us, I'm legally allowed to drive this." He was trying to keep my mind off us moving. I appreciated it; however, it wasn't working.

As we passed between the tall towers of the castle, my entire body tensed. Magic flew from me, making the normal fog that appeared around the island, thicker, darker. The light on the boat was on. It wouldn't allow us to see too far ahead but it was enough.

Paxton sat behind the wheel like he was meant for this. We were close enough that I could see his smile. It helped knowing he was the one beside me while we did this.

The boat turned right, and my breath froze in my lungs. I didn't see anything beyond us, which meant no one could see us. We didn't stay near the island as we went, so I wasn't sure how far the cloak around it encompassed. Paxton kept giving me reassuring smiles and eventually I released the breath I was holding. I didn't breathe easy. Far from it. But I didn't tell Paxton to head back.

We came back to the entryway. Paxton slowed the boat to a stop. "Do you want to go around again?"

Every part of my body was strung tight. Any longer, I worried I'd shatter into a million pieces. "No."

"Okay. Let's head back."

As soon as the boat was back where it usually was, I was out of it and striding toward the castle. I didn't stop until I was in my bathroom with my hands gripping the counter tightly. My breath was coming too fast. My chest heaving from it.

Paxton eventually came up behind me and rubbed his hand up and down my spine. "You did good."

I swung around, anger licking through me. "I shouldn't be like this. I shouldn't need soothing after going on a fucking boat." I turned and faced the shower, not wanting Paxton to see the tears burning my eyes.

"Theo..."

"Why do you want to be with me? I'm pathetic. I'm stuck on this island because I don't have balls big enough to face my fears. I'm weak." My hands fisted by my sides, itching to be pushed through the glass before me.

I should be the strong one. The person who went with Paxton every trip to the mainland. I should watch over him. Make sure no one fucked with him. I should have been there that first supply run when he was assaulted. Instead, I was here, pacing like a child waiting for him to return.

"I don't see you that way." His voice was steady and calm. He wasn't reacting to my tone. "What you did today was brave. You took a step forward."

"Because you were with me. If you hadn't been, I would have stayed inside. Hell, if you hadn't come here that day instead of Leven, I would have starved before I would have tried to get to land and find food. I can swim well. This castle is my prison."

Paxton moved around until he was in front of me. "This castle is your home. Mine too. Every time I come back from a supply run; I feel the warmth of this place inviting me in. It's because of you. Where you are is where I'll be. I don't care if it's here or somewhere else. But this is home, and I love it."

He reached behind himself and turned on the shower. Steam quickly filled the space while we stared at one another. "Before we go in there and I show you just how proud of you I am on my knees, I'd like you to do it again tomorrow."

"You want me to step foot on that boat again?" He couldn't be serious.

"I do. I've worked through my own shit, and I realized that by facing my fears, I was making myself stronger. Now, I wouldn't ask you to do something that would put you in danger. Us motoring around the castle so slowly fish pass us isn't hazardous. The more you do it, the more you'll relax, hopefully."

"And what if I'm not like you? What if I freak the fuck out worse tomorrow?"

"Then we stop. We talk."

"Why do you want me to go out there, Pax?"

"Because I want you to live your life again. I want you to see what you're missing. And I want the world to see the man I do."

"They'll hate me."

"They don't know you."

I shook my head. "They don't need to. My name alone is enough."

"If, and this is a big if, I can convince you to go to Sparkling, we'll do it while you're under disguise. No one will recognize you. Wear a hat, sunglasses. You'll blend right in. I just want you to see everything."

Words stuck in my throat about how I wasn't missing anything by staying here, but they were lies. I missed a lot. The world continued to evolve while I was stuck here. And I was stuck. It was my own fault. Paxton was trying to help me with something I didn't often voice. Something I kept inside. A vision of walking among people again. The way I did when I was a child.

He didn't let me stay trapped in my head. He stripped me of my clothes then did the same to himself. He took my hand and pulled me into the shower. And just like he said, he dropped to his knees in front of me and took my dick deep into his mouth until it was touching his throat.

Any thoughts fled. I was focused on feeling. The way he touched me, tasted me. Paxton made everything else disappear. It was exactly what I needed, and he knew it.

I wasn't sure I'd ever fully deserve this man, but I damn sure wasn't going to take him for granted. He was everything good in my life. The sun I never let fully shine down on me. The warmth I didn't rejoice in outside. He gave me things I never thought I'd have. I hoped I did the same for him. No, we didn't get to do what most couples did. I didn't take him on dates. Didn't show him off to my family and friends. But that didn't make what we were doing any less. It worked for us. For now at least. I wasn't foolish enough to think this life as we lived it would work forever.

Paxton was the reason I got on that boat. Paxton was the reason I'd do it again tomorrow. Because he was my light and I'd let him pull me from the dark.

17

PAXTON

Theo had successfully gotten on the boat two more times. The first was two loops around the island. The second we went farther out until we couldn't see it anymore. Not that we could see much with the way he cloaked us.

Today, we were heading to the coast. It wasn't a supply run, just us seeing how far we could go. Every time Theo was on the boat it got easier for him. I wouldn't say he was comfortable. He tolerated it. Yesterday there was hardly any panic in him by the time we got back. I even got half of a smile out of him when I reminded him how proud I was. He didn't want to hear it, not the praise. Because to Theo, it was nothing to be proud of. He was still getting the praise though.

In a pair of jeans and a T-shirt, Theo slipped on sunglasses and a nondescript baseball hat before getting in the boat. He didn't need me to hold his hand. He did this on his own. I'd never witnessed something so amazing as him learning how to face his fears.

"To the mainland and back?" he asked.

"Yes."

I started the boat and took control, not wanting the magic to

The Ostin Heir

do it for me since this wasn't as simple as going to the pier. That was the goal; however, if Theo wasn't doing well, I would need to get us back fast.

The boat made the smooth glide through the water, between the high spires of the castle. No matter how many times I came and went, that sight always took my breath away. I understood how Theo's view of this place was mixed, but it mesmerized me.

When we were learning about the Ostins in school, it was rumored that the island had crumbled and was gone. There were even search parties who dove into the water, but no evidence was ever found. Little did they know it was there the entire time, hidden by a mage. Covered in fog and shadows from its only surviving member. I didn't put two and two together when I came here the first time. It wasn't even in my head as the boat neared. Then again, that first time held a lot of fear of the unknown for me.

I didn't steer us to the pier right away. I wanted to ease Theo into it. So, we did a lap close to the castle. One farther out. Then we started heading away. Theo tensed. I didn't reach out and try to soothe him, not sure how much physical contact he wanted.

But his hand reached over and landed on my thigh. I relished the feel of it. Theo didn't initiate touch as much as I did. It was usually me placing a hand on his arm when we were talking or putting my palm on his back when we were standing close. It felt so natural, which was weird for me considering I hadn't been that way with anyone else.

The farther we got away from the island, the thinner the fog got. Theo could keep it over us but then, as we approached the pier, it would look odd having that fog only around our boat.

I could see Sparkling in the distance, its brighter beach, sun beating down on the people who were no doubt enjoying the day. We were still closer to Desolate. It was where my heart was. Now that I knew Theo, I wondered if I'd always felt connected to it because of him. I didn't believe in fate, though this certainly made me curious about it.

Leaning closer to Theo, I slowed the boat down to a stop. "You can make out Desolate from here," I told him, pointing toward the beach. The buildings were on the other side of the low-lying fog. The tops were visible, hollowed out shells that they were.

Theo looked at them, seeing them for the first time since that awful day. I watched as the shadows he could easily cast dropped down over his face in a different way. He was shutting down before my eyes.

I moved so I was in his line of sight, standing now while the boat idled. "Look at me."

Theo kept his gaze on my stomach, so I used my hand to draw his chin up. Those eyes I loved had hurt swimming in them.

"Remember what I told you about Desolate? How I always liked going there?"

He nodded.

"It's not all bad, Theo. It gave me a place to be when I didn't think anyone in the world cared about me. That beach isn't the same as it once was. Not everyone is meant for the light. Now look over at Sparkling. I know you can't see it well because of the fog, but you see the sun, don't you?"

Theo turned his head, some of those shadows fell away from him. Not all, that wouldn't be the man who had captured my heart. I had a feeling that Theo would always have some shadows over him. "It's bright," he murmured.

"It is." I brushed my fingers down along his stubbled cheek. "It's been a long time since you felt the sun on your face."

He nodded again and blinked a few times.

"Do you want to feel it again?"

"Yes," he choked out.

"Okay, then let's go. I'll move slow and we'll stop at the pier. We won't get out. Then we'll turn around."

I sat back down and made the rest of the trip. Theo found my thigh again and held on. I wasn't looking ahead when we broke through the fog. I was focused on Theo.

He tipped his head back so the sun could kiss his cheeks, nose, lips, and chin. He didn't show any outward expression about how it felt, but he squeezed my thigh.

It had been seventy years since this man allowed himself to feel that warmth. Something that was normal and natural to the rest of us. All that time he spent on the island, scared, worried he'd succumb to the blood craze. My heart broke when I thought about it. I was grateful he had Leven though. Without him, Theo would have died with no food or blood.

We kept going until we got to the pier. There was another boat docked near us, no one in it. I maneuvered our boat into place and let it idle where Theo could see the sand, the people, the buildings behind them. How happy they were. I was hoping he could picture this as something he could enjoy one day. The warmth of the sand between his toes. Sun shining down on him as he lounged back on a towel.

As much as Desolate always called to me, I saw Sparkling in a new way now. I wasn't the same man I was when I met Leven. I wasn't stuck in an endless cycle of working, eating, and trying to keep myself safe. I had Theo and he made me happier than I'd ever thought was possible.

I looked over to tell him as much, wanting to share my thoughts with him, but when I did, I noticed how tight his features were. How tense his shoulders had gotten. His grip on my thigh was still strong. That hadn't changed.

"Theo?" I spoke low enough where no one would hear us.

"I want to leave," he said through clenched teeth.

"Okay, do you want to talk first? Tell me what happened?" Maybe I could help him through whatever was going on.

"Now," he barked out. It made me jump in my seat.

I quickly maneuvered the boat away and started back toward the island. I'd gotten used to Theo's moods and his anger. He had trouble processing some things still and I'd give him space. There was none of that to be had while we were on the boat. So, I stayed quiet and kept us moving toward the place he said was his prison, yet I knew it was more than that. It was the only place Theo felt comfortable.

Back in the fog, it quickly thickened and encompassed us with a force that had my hair blowing back from my face. Theo hunched forward, dropping his elbows to his knees and his head to his hands. I wanted to reach for him, to remind him I was right here. Instead, I didn't do anything but drive the boat.

The moment we were surrounded by the island, the boat next to the landing, Theo shot from it and moved quickly toward the castle. Shadows followed, telling me he wasn't doing well. I knew this would be hard for him, but I had so much hope once I saw the way he reacted when the sun hit his face. I didn't know what triggered him. It could have been the noise from the beach. The people there. They wouldn't recognize him. Couldn't. Hell, they'd have no idea he was a vampire at all.

I took care of the boat and made my way inside, looking around for Theo. I didn't check his bedroom until last. It was almost like I was avoiding what would happen when I found him. Of course, he'd be in there. It was either that or the library, which was empty.

His door was closed when I walked down the hall. I stood in front of it, not sure what to do. I wanted to be in there with him, holding him, helping him through this. It was clear he didn't want me there or else he would have left the door open.

The Ostin Heir

Letting out a breath, I went to my room and didn't close the door behind me. I opened my windows before flopping back onto the bed to stare at the ceiling.

I wasn't sure how long I lay there before I got up and went in search of something to eat. Theo still hadn't left his room; he might not for the rest of the night. I wished he would though.

As I was eating a sandwich, I sat at the dining table, angry at myself for pushing him. I shouldn't have done it. I was trying to get him to live a full life again, but he already was on the island. His life didn't look like mine, and I had to remember that. Yes, he said he wanted to try and gain his freedom. To live like he used to. To see if he could. He didn't need to do it with the speed I was pushing him though.

My head was a mess of worry while I made him a sandwich and put it in the fridge, hoping he'd come down at some point to eat. I washed my dishes, swallowed down another glass of water before cleaning that as well, and made my way back upstairs.

Theo's door was still closed when I walked past. The solid wood could have been steel for the way it felt, like there was so much separating us. This impenetrable wall between Theo and me. I hoped he hadn't built that security back up around his heart after today. I hoped I didn't ruin everything we had. Nothing else mattered to me but that man.

It was when I was back in my bed, changed into cotton shorts and a T-shirt, curled up on my side that I realized I wasn't falling for him anymore. I'd gone and truly given him my heart.

Sleep started to claim me, making my eyelids droop, and my body go lax. The last thing I thought of was Theo and how much I loved him.

18

THEO

I sat in my bedroom, tucked in the corner with the open windows to my left like I could keep part of Paxton with me that way. The door to my bedroom was across from me, in my line of sight. My knees were pulled up; my arms wrapped around them. I fucked up. I was weak. Couldn't even sit on the boat and look at the beach I once played on as a child that was now separated by a thick dividing line of my own creation.

The way the fog and darkness completely encompassed the ocean rolling to the beach of Desolate was hard to watch. I could have removed it. Pulled it away to let the sun shine down like it did on Sparkling, but I didn't because that darkness felt like it was part of my very soul.

Desolate and Sparkling. I stopped calling them their old names long ago and only knew them by those names now. The way Paxton looked at Desolate with longing made me hate myself even more by keeping him in this castle. He could leave but he wouldn't. For some fucked-up reason he liked being here with me. And I'd gone and become an asshole instead of thanking him for trying to help me.

I rocked slightly, wondering if I would ever be able to func-

The Ostin Heir

tion with the rest of society again. If they'd even want me to. It wasn't like I was a stand-up citizen, not with the past my family created. A legacy I never wanted but was destined to suffer with.

The floor became my friend as I sat there long into the night. Eventually, the room lightened, not like the sun that had warmed my face the day before. No, I wasn't feeling that. This was sunlight shrouded by fog and haze.

The sun... It had been so long since I felt that. It was my own fault. I could brush away the fog with a wave of my hand. Let the sun highlight the castle like it had in the past. But I didn't deserve it. Didn't think I was worthy of such a gift.

And here I sat in the same spot when I finally heard Paxton leave his bedroom and stop outside mine. I'd thought he'd walk past like he did yesterday, but he didn't. He knocked. It was soft, hesitant. I made Paxton that way. His vibrant smile was most likely gone, instead worry would be in its place.

My body was locked up tight from staying in the same position so long. I couldn't turn him away, not when I felt like I needed him to breathe.

"Come in," I said, no real emotion in my voice. I was choking it down to the best of my ability. If I let it bubble up, I would break.

The door slowly opened, revealing Paxton on the other side. He was sleep rumpled with his hair mussed and his shirt and shorts wrinkled. He didn't have dark circles under his eyes, telling me he got some sleep. He was here, never wavering, for me.

He saw me from where he stood. My body tensed waiting for the blow. For him to see me like this and tell me I wasn't worth it. But he didn't. He came forward and sat down directly in front of me before reaching forward and pulling me into his arms. He held me. Kissed my head. Rocked with me.

The dam broke. My face was pressed to his shoulder. I let out a muffled sob as my body started shaking with the force of emotion that hit me. I pushed it down all night and now I couldn't stop it if I wanted to. Tears ran from my eyes, down my cheeks, soaking Paxton's shirt. I clutched to him, fisted the fabric at his chest, never wanting to let go. And he never asked me to. He held me through it all.

It felt like an hour had passed before I was finally able to get ahold of myself, though in reality, it wasn't that long.

"We never have to go on the boat again," Paxton said quietly.

I shook my head and pulled back. I was sure my eyes were bloodshot, and I looked like hell. "I didn't go through this to give up." I wanted to. I wanted to tell Paxton I wasn't leaving this island again, but I couldn't do that because I wanted this life with him and staying here every day of every month for every year wasn't truly living.

"I can't watch this happen to you over and over. It's killing me, Theo, to know you're hurting like this."

"I'd understand if it was too much."

"Never. I knew who you were when I said I wanted to be with you. That hasn't changed."

"You're too good for me."

He gave me a lopsided smile. "You have it wrong. You think because you have some shit to work through that I'm better. Remember who you are. You're the Ostin heir. The king of your family."

I scoffed. "What family?"

"Me, Theo."

"Goddammit, Pax. Why do you have to be so sweet?"

"Just telling the truth."

"I'm not a suitable partner for you."

"You're perfect. Strong. Capable."

The Ostin Heir

"I'm pathetic."

"You're not."

"I'm—"

Paxton leaned forward and kissed me, effectively silencing the words on my lips. He didn't linger. Just enough to shut me up. He pulled back and asked, "Are you hungry? I doubt you left this room all night."

My stomach growled, answering for me.

Paxton smiled again and stood, holding out his hand for me. I took it, letting him lift me up. How many times would he have to do that? Pull me out of this hell I created for myself? It shouldn't be this way. I should be the strong one for him. Be everything he needed, yet I was curled in a ball on the floor all night because I couldn't handle my shit.

A gentle hand on my cheek brought my eyes to his. "Stop," he told me. "I can guess where your mind went. Trust me when I say I want this—you—all of it." Trust him, yes. I did so easily. Believing he really wanted to be here was something entirely different.

Downstairs in the kitchen, Paxton started pulling things from the refrigerator to make us breakfast. I saw the plate there with the sandwich on it. I retrieved it.

"Did you make this for me?" I asked.

He nodded while he took out a couple of pans from a cabinet. "I wanted you to have something to eat if you came downstairs."

Tears started to build in my eyes, but I blinked them back. The last time I cried this much was when I lost Leven. Before that it was when I lost my parents.

With the plate in hand, I took off the plastic wrap and lifted the sandwich to my mouth.

"You don't have to eat that," Paxton said. "It's probably soggy from the mayonnaise soaking into the bread."

My mouth was full, but I still got out, "Don't care." I didn't. The sandwich was soggy, but it was also damn good to my empty stomach. Besides, Paxton made it, therefore I would eat it. Simple as that.

Paxton smiled while he whisked together scrambled eggs. He cooked as I ate the rest of my sandwich then grabbed a bag of blood. I was almost out. The next supply run was in six days, and it was also a run for more blood.

The blood was cold as it trickled down my throat. Blood from a vein would be warm if not hot. Even if I thought I wouldn't lose my mind with a blood craze, I didn't think I could drink from someone. I'd fear I'd kill them. Though my family didn't kill each other. They killed humans. Vampires would never get drained dry. Since I didn't know any personally and had no desire to, I was left with the clinical bags to sate my hunger. It worked. I didn't get any pleasure or joy drinking this way.

After throwing the bag in the garbage, I looked up to find Paxton watching me, spatula in hand. He had eggs cooking in one pan and sausage in another. It was almost like he was in a trance. I cocked an eyebrow and waited for him to say something.

He shook his head and turned back to the stove, but not before I noticed a bulge in the front of his cotton shorts. They didn't conceal anything.

Feeling my mood shift now that I ate and drank, I stepped up behind him and slid my arms around his waist. I hoped I wasn't doing anything he didn't want me to. In that moment, I needed to touch him. To feel his warm skin against mine. His body pressed to me.

Paxton leaned back but kept pushing the eggs around the pan. I pressed a kiss to his neck as I lifted his shirt so my hands could brush over his skin. He felt so good. So right. I was addicted to him. If he ever decided to leave, I didn't know what I would do.

He arched his back, pushing his ass into my groin. My dick had already begun plumping up. Now it was hard, insistent where it slotted perfectly between his clothed cheeks. I wished we were naked. I wished I could feel him like that again.

A moan slipped past his lips. "Theo, I'm cooking."

"If you tell me to stop, I will."

"Don't you dare."

I teased along his shorts. Dipped my fingers beneath the waistband of his boxer briefs, brushing the head of his dick where it stood tall, begging for attention. My hand wrapped around it, and I started pumping him.

"Take my shorts off," he said. His head had dropped back against my shoulder. He turned the burners off and pushed the pans to the rear of the stove.

His clothes slid over his hips easier, falling to pool at his feet. He braced his hands on the counter on either side of the stove. "I want you so much, Theo."

I skated my hands over his hips until I found his dick again. One hand went back to jerking him while the other rolled his balls in my palm. All that skin, all that heat, I loved it.

"Take your shorts off," he told me. I didn't mind Paxton telling me what to do, especially when we were like this. It was a far change from when we first met. Then again, I trusted him now. Cared deeply for him. Couldn't imagine my life without him.

Releasing his balls, I pulled my shorts and boxer briefs down one hip at a time until they were on the floor then kicked them off. I leaned forward and slotted my dick back on Paxton's ass, the precum creating a slick trail to glide it over his flesh.

"Fuck me, Theo," Paxton said, his breath coming faster.

Mine froze in my chest. "What?"

He peered over his shoulder. "I want you to fuck me. Please. I need you."

"But we've never... I haven't..." I couldn't get a full sentence out. He was standing before me, offering me something no one had before. It was a gift. One I didn't take lightly. After what Paxton had been through, been hurt by the hands of others, he was trusting me to take care of him. And I would. I'd never hurt him.

19

PAXTON

When I thought about the day Theo would slip deep inside me, I didn't think it would be in the kitchen with the scent of eggs and sausage in the air, the stove still hot, and my hands planted on the counter while my ass stuck out in clear invitation.

But that was where I was, and it felt perfect. Because it was Theo.

I also understood what this meant for him. He'd never had sex before. Didn't know what it felt like to do this. Then again, I'd never had sex with anyone I loved. The times I had sex; I was forced into it. No. That had no part in my thoughts right now. I wasn't living in the past anymore. I wasn't waking up to a nightmare that felt like it wouldn't end. This man was special, and I was going to show him how much he meant to me.

There used to be a part of me, a big one, that worried when I eventually did fall in love I wouldn't be able to have this with them. That I'd flashback. I knew if I did with Theo, he'd understand, and maybe that was why this was easier. Theo would never push me to do something I didn't want to. With that knowledge came so much trust. And a freedom to let go of everything. To not think but to feel, like I'd done to him that night when I pushed the dildo into his ass and made him come.

A moan crawled up my throat thinking about that night, making me even harder. Theo was behind me, sliding his thick length between my cheeks, but not trying to breach me. Simply gliding.

"Tell me what to do," he said.

"Do we have lube down here?"

"No, but don't move. I'll be right back."

He left the room, and I was standing with my clothes still bunched at my ankles. I kicked them off then got rid of my shirt too. I also shifted over so my face wasn't near the hot stove. If I really got into this and bent forward, I didn't want to burn my head. I had Theo's blood in me, keeping me healthy. I'd heal from a burn, but it would still hurt.

We didn't need condoms. Theo couldn't give me any diseases and vice versa. Plus, it was Theo. I wanted to feel every inch of him bare inside me.

Theo came back with his dick in hand as he stroked it, glistening with lube already and the tube in the other hand.

"Someone's impatient." I smirked.

"Someone has never had sex before and you're spread out in front of me like a fantasy I've had all of my life." He came up behind me, draped his body over mine, and wrapped his arms around me. His slick dick nestled back into place. "I always wanted the kind of love my parents shared. I remember how they looked at each other. How they cared, cherished, loved. I wanted that. And here you are."

"A dream come true," I murmured. He was for me too. I didn't think I'd ever get to have this.

"I don't dream but I understand the saying."

I looked over my shoulder at him. His face was close to mine. "You don't dream?"

"No. I was the only one in my family never to have one. No one knew why."

"Interesting."

"Yes, but so is this..." His slick finger trailed down my crevice to my hole. "I remember what you did to me. Is that what I do to you? Tell me how you like it."

"I've played with myself recently. I won't be as tight. You'll still need to stretch me. Work me up from one finger to three then I'll be good."

"Okay." He pressed a kiss to my shoulder then hesitated. "Thank you for this, Paxton."

"Never thank me for something this amazing."

"But I must. You're a gift."

"You're giving as much to me."

His finger breached me, causing me to tense. The first push in usually did that to me. It was the bite of pain that quickly melted away to pleasure. I forced myself to relax, not wanting Theo to think he was doing something wrong.

He stretched me until I was jerking myself, begging him to get inside.

"I'm bigger than my fingers," he said, concern evident.

"You are, but my body will adjust. Just go slow and use a good amount of lube."

Theo lubed me some more. Then the blunt head of his dick pushed against my rim. I widened my stance, pushed back as he went forward until the head popped through and was inside me. Theo paused, stroked his hand up and down my spine while the other kept a firm grip on my hip. He pushed more, kept going this time, achingly slow, until he was fully inside me, his body flush to mine.

"Holy shit," he whispered.

"I know." I hung my head between my arms, grateful I wasn't near the stove any longer.

"Can I move?"

"Yes, I want that."

Theo pulled back and thrust in. It was this sensual glide of his body into mine. Each time he pushed forward; a small gasp left my lips. I felt like it was on fire but in the best way. I knew once Theo started fucking me, his body would take over and would know what to do. And, fuck, did he do it well.

The room filled with our panted breaths, the sound of skin slapping skin, and the smell of sex. It was intoxicating. It amped up the entire experience. We could be as loud as we wanted since there was no one to hear us, yet we both kept quiet. It was like if we spoke, we'd break this spell we were under.

"Pax, I can't..." he groaned out.

"Touch me. I want to feel you everywhere."

He was covering me again, wrapping his bigger body around mine, making me feel safe. If I ever needed it, it was right now when I was completely vulnerable. Not just with my body but with my heart too. Every thrust felt like Theo was claiming more of me. More of my very soul.

His hand gripped my dick. It took a minute for him to find his rhythm between his thrusts and his hand, but he did, and then they were perfectly timed.

"Yes, more," I begged him. "Harder, Theo."

He didn't ask if I was sure; he simply did it. Gave me what I needed. His hand sped up; my eyes slammed closed.

Then I felt the graze of something sharp on my skin where my neck met my shoulder. "Theo?"

"I won't bite you. I promise. I'd never do that without asking. I just wanted to feel you like this." His voice broke at the end.

If I was a vampire, he could drink from me. He could finally know what it felt like to do so.

"I trust you," I told him.

He groaned. His fangs dragged along my skin. His hand tightened on my dick, and two thrusts later I screamed out his name as I came. Stars danced behind my eyelids. My body strung tight, and I shot all over the cabinets, not giving a shit about them. Nothing else mattered but Theo and me.

His hips stuttered, losing their rhythm. He was close.

"Come, Theo. Give it to me. I want it."

He slammed into me, pushing me forward, my feet trying to stay in place. But Theo was an animal as he chased his release. "Fuck, Pax, fuck!" He pushed in once more, his fingers bruising my hips, and came. I felt the tremors wracking his body. He was so hot and hard inside me. I knew I'd be sore until I healed, but holy shit was it worth it.

Sweat dripped from Theo onto my back, slicking my skin more than it already was. We were filthy and I reveled in it. Both of us stayed there for a moment until our breaths started to slow.

His forehead dropped to the top of my spine as his arms fully engulfed me once more. "Paxton..."

Pushing up from the counter, I turned slowly, letting his dick slip from my body. I peered into those eyes of his, which seemed darker than I thought was possible. I pressed my lips to his, needing to taste him after what we just experienced together.

He held me tight. His tongue pushed between my lips, and we just kissed. Nothing more but it was everything. This entire thing was.

Eventually I broke the kiss, needing to come up for air and we rested our foreheads together. "You were... I don't have words," I said.

"I love you, Paxton. So, fucking much. I'm so damn scared but I had to tell you how I feel."

Leaning back, I saw the truth of his words in his eyes. Hell, I felt them while we were having sex. Hearing them was completely different, unexpected. "I love you too."

"God, Pax." He kissed me again, chaste this time. "Please don't leave me. I don't think I'd survive it."

It was my turn to hold on to him like my life depended on it. To grip him tightly so he'd know I wasn't going anywhere. "Never, Theo. I'm right where I want to be."

I meant it. I wasn't going anywhere. With that thought came the knowledge that I had a big decision to make about my life. If I was going to spend it with him, not that either of us had said that, but I had a feeling Theo wasn't the type to bail when the going got tough, then I needed to seriously consider extending my life beyond what those drops of Theo's blood did to me. I needed to start to seriously consider having him change me into a vampire like him. Then when his fangs dragged along my skin, he could drink from me. Get his nourishment. No longer needing to buy blood.

There was no point in voicing that out loud yet. I wasn't ready to and didn't want to rush into such an important decision. It wasn't like I had family to consider elsewhere. It was only me. But *I* was important. *I* mattered. So, I would take however long I needed until I was sure it was what I wanted.

"I think we have to heat up breakfast," he said, lips pressed against my temple.

I chuckled. "You're probably right. Now I'm really hungry." Stepping back, the movement caused the evidence of what we just did to slip from my ass and down my inner thighs. "I need to clean up."

Theo spun me around and gripped my ass.

"What are you doing?"

"I want to see." He dropped to his knees behind me.

"Jesus, Theo." I wasn't sure if I wanted to turn away out of embarrassment or spread my legs and let him look his fill. When I felt his finger glide over my skin, my decision was made. He could do whatever the hell he wanted back there, and I'd welcome it.

"I was inside you, Pax."

"Yeah, I seem to remember that."

"Smart-ass."

His fingers glided down my ass, over my rim, and down my thighs. He worked his way back up, pushing his fingers inside when he got to my hole again. I was sore. There was a bit of a sting, but then he moved his fingers and I moaned in response.

"You're mine, Paxton."

"Yours. Anything. Everything."

His tongue licked around where his fingers were. I fell forward but was able to catch myself with my hands on my knees.

"Fuck, Theo!"

I'd never felt anything like that before. He hummed behind me, kept licking like he was cleaning me up. My body was shaking by the time he stood again, my dick halfway hard.

Theo lifted me in his arms and took us to the dining room where he dropped into a chair, his bare ass meeting the wood. He settled me on his lap then sliced into his wrist with his fang. Blood pooled on his skin. "Drink from me." He held his wrist out.

I didn't hesitate. I'd grown addicted to the cinnamon flavor of his blood. My tongue licked along his skin. My lips latched on and sucked once. I didn't need a lot, but he was delicious.

My dick went fully hard. I was about to pull away when he pressed his wrist in place and started stroking my dick with his other hand. I licked, moved my hips to fuck his hand. And came so fast I didn't have time to do anything but moan against his wrist.

If this was what happened when we had sex, we were doing this all the time.

20

THEO

I was on the boat again. We went to the mainland yesterday once more, just to get me used to it. We didn't get off the boat. I didn't want to give up, no matter how many times Paxton said it was okay if I couldn't go through with it.

Today, we were making a supply run. We were low on food and other things. Blood was gone. There was no turning back. Maybe that was what I needed to complete the trip. The fact that without it, I wouldn't have the blood I needed.

Paxton had been good about talking to me the entire trip to the mainland. He didn't stop so I could see things. The boat stayed at the same speed until the pier was in sight. My body was tense; my blunt fingernails dug into my palms as I fisted my hands. I was doing this. I was on the boat. We came all this way. There was no backing out.

The boat did what it was supposed to, thanks to the magic, and brought us right to the pier. Paxton didn't need to drive this time.

He turned to me. "Are you ready?" I was glad he didn't ask if I was okay. I couldn't lie to him and didn't want to worry him more than he already was.

I nodded, not trusting my words to come out firm like there was no doubt in my mind I could handle this. There were many, many doubts. But Paxton didn't need me to voice them. He had to already be aware.

He held his hand out for mine when he stood. "I'll be by your side the whole time. Remember, this is simply getting our supplies and heading home. Eye on the prize." Before we left, he said he'd get on his knees for me again when we got back. That was all the prize I needed. Paxton's gorgeous gaze on me as he swallowed my dick.

I looked at the gangway that would lead us to the top of the pier. "How many trips do you make to bring everything to the boat?"

"Not many anymore. Zeke helps. He carries as much as I do."

Paxton told me at first, he was worried about someone stealing from Zeke's car, but Zeke was sure to lock it every time they stepped away. Zeke had also become a friend to Paxton. They had lunch on the supply runs now. The man didn't ask too many questions. Didn't pry into Paxton's life. Zeke said if Paxton wanted him to know something, he'd tell him. And for his part, Paxton had been vague. Merely saying he had a large boat that he lived on with his boyfriend and that he used this smaller one to replenish what he needed. Zeke believed him. Or maybe he didn't. Either way, he was always here for Paxton.

I made sure my sunglasses and hat were firmly in place before ascending the gangway behind Paxton. My first step onto the pier had me frozen to the wood. There were people there. Not too many but enough where I felt like they were watching me. Staring. Judging. Trying to figure out who I was. I didn't look a lot like my father. I had his dark hair and eyes. Strong jaw. But those were also common features of others.

The Ostin Heir

There was nothing to tie me to him that these people would recognize.

Warm fingers wrapped around my hand, pulling me out of my head and to the man in front of me. Paxton filled my line of sight.

"You and me," he reminded me.

I nodded.

Together, we put one foot in front of the other and started the walk down the pier. Every plank my booted feet met felt like I was walking to my death. Sweat ran down my back. This was a nervous sweat. One that spoke of how badly I felt.

When we got to the end of the pier, more people walked around, coming and going from the beach. There was a large parking lot where they were unloading or reloading their cars. But there was also a car with a man leaning against the trunk smiling.

I was grateful for all the things Leven used to bring me from the mainland. Magazines, newspapers. It made what I was seeing easier, not a huge adjustment. Things changed quickly. Technology improved. Cars became more modern, sleek. Leven had talked about getting one but never followed through on it. He used a cab for years. Then apps became a thing as well as requesting a ride on them. Leven enjoyed that. Was able to talk to different people when in the car with them. He was the type of person who could make friends no matter where he went.

"Let me introduce you to Zeke." Paxton smiled and it warmed me. Helped relieve a bit of the tension. Not much because I had a feeling that wouldn't go away until I was home. Knowing Paxton was here helped.

Zeke had light brown hair that was parted on one side and combed back on the other. The sides weren't much shorter, but enough to keep the cut neat. His face was clean-shaven. Eyes crinkled slightly at the corners. This wasn't a fake smile. It was one of friendship. I didn't get the feeling Zeke wanted more with Paxton than that. And Paxton assured me there was no interest on either side. That didn't stop me from gripping his hand tighter. He was mine and anxiety about coming on the mainland or not, I would fight for him.

"Zeke, hi," Paxton greeted. "This is Theo." We decided to go with my real first name since otherwise I probably wouldn't respond if he was talking to me. Also, it was a common name. Nothing that should pique anyone's attention.

"I get to meet the boyfriend finally," Zeke said and held out his hand for mine. "It's nice to put a face to you. Paxton talks about you every time I see him."

Since Paxton's hand was in my left one, I wiped my clammy right hand on my thigh before offering it to Zeke. "It's nice to meet you." We shook briefly.

My breath came fast. I hadn't met another person like this since Paxton arrived on the island and that was different. I had to make a good impression here. This was someone Paxton could count on when he came to the mainland. Someone who drove him away when his asshole neighbor was trying to hurt him.

Paxton released my hand and put his on the small of my back, moving himself closer to me. His lips brushed my jaw then he whispered, "You're doing great. We're going to get our supplies now."

"Ready to go?" Zeke asked.

"Yup," Paxton replied.

We got into the car with Paxton close to me, his hand on my thigh. I tried focusing on him at first but couldn't keep my gaze off the buildings outside my window. In the car I felt different. The ride was smooth. It was also like I was in a cocoon, a buffer from the outside world. I didn't bother trying to figure out the electronics inside. There were too many dials, numbers, things I didn't care about right now. No, I had to focus on what was outside and try to regulate my breathing. I wasn't a stranger to anxiety, but I didn't live with it daily either. It only appeared when Paxton left the island or when I did with him.

The first stop we made was the grocery store, which was nothing like I remembered it when I was a child. Then again, nothing was. Paxton made it as painless as possible for me. He told me I could stay in the car with Zeke, but I refused to. I always wanted Paxton by my side, not only because he helped me through this but because I didn't know if there would be someone who wanted to harm him nearby. I wasn't of much use, but now that I was here, I could protect him.

The store was too loud, too bright, and had too many options for food. It took everything in me not to use my magic and shadow out some of the lights on the ceiling. Instead, I kept my head down, the brim of the hat provided some cover from the harsh lights. I took off my sunglasses when we got inside since Paxton said it would probably draw more attention to me if I left them on.

I kept one hand on the cart as he picked out the food we needed. I felt like the family we passed in one aisle where the child kept his fingers hooked on the metal rungs of the cart while his mother shopped.

"Do you want to pick out some things?" Paxton asked.

"No, I want to get out of here."

He pressed a kiss to my temple and kept us moving.

Every time I dared to glance up, no one was watching us, even if I felt like every eye in the store was on me. It was difficult to keep walking when all I wanted to do was run outside and hide in the comfort of Zeke's car. I was weak. This proved it. Couldn't even shop in a store like a regular person.

Paxton kept talking to me as we shopped. He was trying to

keep my mind off of things. I appreciated it but it didn't work. I became enamored with the floor beneath my feet as we went through each aisle. When we went to the section where there were doors with the frozen foods behind them, I was grateful every time Paxton opened one of them. The cold air seeped out, chilling the sweat coating my skin.

By the time we got to the line to pay for our food, I was nearly vibrating with need to get out of the store. Luckily, the line was short. I didn't care about the sounds the register made. It was new to me. Could be interesting if I stopped panicking long enough to look.

I heard Paxton tell the woman thank you and we were moving again. Finally. I needed to get the fuck out of here.

Outside, I took a deep breath and resisted bending over at the waist to put my hands on my knees. That would surely draw attention. "Holy shit," I said when I felt like I could breathe again. I put the sunglasses back over my eyes.

Zeke was waiting inside his car with it running to keep the cool air on. We stopped next to the trunk.

Paxton's arms came around me. He held me tight. "I love you, Theo. You did great in there. I know it wasn't easy, but I'm so fucking proud of you."

Emotion choked me as I held on to Paxton like I'd drown if I let go.

"Everything okay?" I heard Zeke ask.

"Yeah, we're good," Paxton said.

I helped them put the groceries in the trunk then we were on our way again. We only had one more stop to make at Novus's shop for my blood. Paxton wanted to keep this trip as simple as possible. I wasn't going in with him.

Mages could live a long time. They had spells, potions, no doubt vampire blood they drank. Things that kept them alive much longer than Leven was. He saw Novus the whole time he was on the island with me, and Paxton went to the same one. If I went in there, I thought she'd recognize me, so I stayed put in the air-conditioned car. It was something I greatly appreciated. We didn't have it on the island. Didn't need it. The stone kept the castle cool as did the sea breeze. And in the winters, when the air was much colder, we had fireplaces that didn't need fresh wood or gas to keep them lit. My magic did that. The castle held the warmth well.

The shop Novus had was small and eccentric. There were crystals lining the windows, along with little bottles and even a few skulls. There were signs advertising healing potions and spells to curse someone. Mages were accepted in the world like vampires were, but they weren't elevated to the level of the royal vampire families. Paxton told me humans went in there often while he was buying blood, looking around, joking about what they found. They knew mages could do things, but it was widely thought of as a joke, which was foolish on the human's part. Mages could destroy them, but they didn't. They lived a peaceful life, making their livings off the vampires and others who were serious when they requested their services.

Paxton emerged with a nondescript canvas bag that I knew held an ice pack and the blood I needed. To the outsider, it looked like nothing suspicious. He didn't put this in the trunk, instead kept it with us in the cabin of the car to keep it cool.

"Back to the pier?" Zeke asked.

Paxton smiled at his friend, who was looking at him in the rearview mirror. "Yes, please. Time to get home."

"One day you'll tell me what you buy in there. I've never been inside." He scrunched up his nose as he looked at the storefront. "Is it like voodoo?"

"No, it's not like voodoo." Paxton laughed. "You should read up on mages. They're very smart and can do a lot."

"If you say so." I wasn't surprised Zeke was skeptical. Most humans were.

Paxton slid over and pressed himself to my side as the car started forward. We were almost home. Almost back to where I felt safe and could relax again. Every muscle in my body was still strung tight but we were almost there.

21

PAXTON

The trip to Sparkling and the surrounding area went better than I hoped. Theo did great. He probably thought he didn't, but I watched him. Saw the way he would tense. Felt the squeeze of my hand when something bothered him. But he pushed through.

To most people, running to the store wasn't a big deal. It was part of life. To Theo it felt like a mountain he couldn't climb. Now he could.

Life wasn't easy. I knew that firsthand. Giving up and letting the walls crash around you, hiding you, didn't make anything go away. I had to fight to get my life back. Fight so I wasn't scared to death every time I tried to sleep at night, worried someone was going to come in and hurt me. Chuck and his friends took a lot from me. Now that I no longer lived there, I was free of him and the violence I endured. The violation of my body.

Zeke helped Theo and I carry our things down to the boat. He tried to make conversation with Theo. It didn't work. My vampire just nodded or shook his head. Gave a half-hearted smile here and there. Theo was being as polite as he could.

We said goodbye to Zeke and thanked him for helping us. I tipped him a huge amount. He'd told me repeatedly I didn't have to do that. He even said just to call him when I got here and he'd help me without the app, me not paying a thing, but I didn't feel right about doing that. I was taking up his time so I thought he should be paid. There was the added comfort of having a friend with me. Not a stranger driving me around to run errands.

I hadn't had a friend like Zeke for as long as I could remember. Most people didn't take the time to get to know me. Or if they did, they wanted something from me. That wasn't how friendship should work. Zeke was genuine. A good guy. He listened when I talked. He cared. And I was there for him if he needed to talk as well. When I was here that was, since my phone had no signal out on the island.

Theo and I were moving things around in the boat so we could get seated and start our journey home. He still had his hat and sunglasses on. I saw how his shoulders relaxed once he was back in the boat. I never thought I'd see the thing bring him a measure of comfort.

I waved at Zeke one last time. He returned it with a smile on his face.

A shout from somewhere by the beach caught my attention. I glanced up and saw a man running toward the pier. As he got closer, I realized it was Chuck and his eyes were on me.

"Shit," I said and started moving things around faster. I wanted to get the fuck away from here.

Theo's head snapped up. "What?"

"Chuck. I need to get out of here."

"Chuck?" he growled. I'd never heard him make that noise before.

"Paxton!" Chuck yelled. So much for me hoping he forgot about me.

The Ostin Heir

I ignored him. My hands shook as I took my seat to get the boat started.

Then I heard another noise. A strangled cry. I looked up and saw Chuck had Zeke pinned to the side of his car.

I was about to rush back but Theo was already out of the boat, striding toward the pier. I watched him, mesmerized by the sheer strength in his steps. Gone was the man who feared this trip. Who didn't want anyone to see him, to figure out who he was. Then my mind got with the program, and I chased after him.

"Theo!"

He didn't respond. Chuck had his hand around Zeke's throat. He was saying something I couldn't hear but his gaze was on us. There were others around, not doing a fucking thing to help Zeke. Standing there, watching with wide eyes instead of trying to get Zeke free. Or hell, even calling the cops. They didn't have their phones out. No one was videoing this like they would have if we were somewhere else.

This was Sparkling Beach. Nothing bad happened here. The shit from where I lived next door to Chuck never bled this way. These people lived in a bubble of happiness. They didn't fear for their lives or worry they would be mugged or worse. They didn't know that life. If Theo and I hadn't been here, I wasn't sure if anyone would have bothered to help. Then again, Chuck was targeting Zeke because he saw me. Because Zeke waved to me.

Theo reached them first. I watched as he gripped Chuck's forearm hard until Chuck cried out in pain and let go. Then it was Chuck who was against the car, Theo's forearm pressed to his throat as his body bent backward.

I raced over to Zeke. He was trembling, holding his neck as a tear tracked down his cheek. "Zeke, let me look." He dropped his hand and there was an angry red mark on his skin.

"Touch him again and I'll kill you," Theo seethed. I lifted my gaze and saw Theo was nose to nose with Chuck.

Foolish Chuck didn't back down. "I'll do whatever I fucking please. You don't own him."

"No, but I don't make promises I can't keep." Theo parted his lips. His fangs descended.

Chuck looked down. That was when I saw the fear in his eyes. Something I'd never seen before.

Theo wasn't done talking. "Now that you know what I am, heed my warning. I won't make it again. Next time I'll follow through. You touch him or Paxton and I'll murder you. Not in your sleep. Not in your apartment. When you least fucking expect it. I want you looking over your shoulder for the rest of your pathetic life, wondering if I'm there in the shadows, waiting to end your sad existence."

Chuck's voice shook. "I won't touch them again."

"Don't think I'm not aware of what you did to Paxton. You're lucky you're still fucking breathing after hurting him. I'd call the police but rotting in prison is too good for you. No, I want you to be afraid. I want you to feel what Paxton did. That cold dread every time you step foot outside of your apartment." Theo took a long inhale. "I can smell your fear. You're right to be scared. I can kill you with one squeeze of my hand."

"You can't," Chuck rasped out. "The peace agreement."

Theo laughed humorlessly. "You think I give a shit about that? When it comes to Paxton and Zeke, nothing will keep you safe." Theo released Chuck to grip the back of his neck. He hauled him away from the car, not giving a shit who saw, and shoved him hard to the point that Chuck fell to his hands and knees. With a raised voice, Theo said, "This man is a rapist. An abuser. Stay away from him."

All eyes in the parking lot swung toward Chuck as he

crawled before standing and ran away with his shorts soaked in the crotch.

Theo came back over to Zeke and me but was looking at my friend. "Are you okay?"

Zeke nodded then let out a whimper as the move caused him pain.

"Do you have anywhere you need to be?"

He shook his head. Zeke was on his own like I was before I met Theo. His parents kicked him out as soon as he graduated high school. He had come out as gay to them when he was sixteen. They hardly spoke to him after that. The only time was to demand his presence at events.

Zeke's family had money. A lot of it. They didn't want it to look bad on them if their son left at sixteen. At eighteen it was like he went off to college, not with a car loaded with his things and enough money to rent a hole-in-a-wall apartment. This way they could pretend to their friends he was off living his life, happy. Not miserable trying to survive. They hadn't spoken to him since.

"Gather your things from your car and lock it. You're coming with us. I won't leave you here after that asshole touched you."

Zeke scrambled around to open the door and got what he needed. He closed and locked it. Theo stood by our sides like a sentry.

I took Zeke's arm and led him back to the boat. His body was shaking so I wrapped my arm around him and held him close. I knew what it was like to be on the receiving end of Chuck's hatred.

Theo followed at our backs, his heavy steps sounding out on the wood planks of the pier like rumbles of thunder warning of an impending storm. I didn't release Zeke until he was sitting down on the boat. Theo and I sat. I didn't waste time getting the boat moving again. I didn't use the magic on it. I did it by hand, not wanting anyone to see or hear anything. There were still eyes on us. I could feel them.

What happened just now in the parking lot was so out of the norm for these people. Most of them had probably never seen a violent act except on TV or in the movies. This was real life, and they weren't sure what to do with it. I was all too familiar with this side of things.

It wasn't until we were back on the Desolate side of the sea, where the fog wrapped around us, that I let out a breath. Theo wasn't touching Zeke, but he was offering him words of comfort in his own way.

"I'll kill him if I see him near you again," Theo told him.

Zeke's eyes were huge as he stared at the man I loved. Was he scared of Theo now? I'd never told Zeke what Theo was, who he was. But Theo let his fangs appear in front of Chuck. Zeke had to have seen them too. No one else did around us. Theo and Chuck were too close together.

"He'll bleed slowly for his crimes," Theo added.

"Theo, I think that's enough," I told him. "I know you mean well, but I don't think it's helping Zeke at the moment."

Theo muffled a curse. "I'm sorry. I've never threatened anyone's life like that before."

I couldn't help but laugh because honestly if I didn't, I was going to cry. Now that we were away from everyone, a flashback of the last time I saw Chuck was at the forefront of my mind. I shook the thought away. "Theo means well," I said to Zeke. "He doesn't have the same social skills you and I do. This is him protecting us in his own way."

Theo nodded but didn't say anything else.

This was a clusterfuck of epic proportions. Chuck had shown up. Hurt Zeke. Theo in turn threatened Chuck. Exposed what he was. And now Zeke was on our boat, heading back to the castle, where we would have some serious explaining to do. The only bright spot was that we were safe, and no one was following us. No one knew where we went thanks to the island being hidden.

How much Theo wanted to tell Zeke was up to him, though the moment Zeke saw the castle, he'd have more questions. I wasn't going to say anything. I'd let Theo lead.

The fog thickened the closer we got to the island. I had the way memorized. The pendants Theo and I both wore had the island appearing before us. Tall spires. Towers. That waterway in between.

Zeke gasped. This was just the tip of the iceberg. By the time Theo was done talking to him, we'd have to pick his jaw up off the floor.

22

THEO

The decision to bring Zeke here was rolling over in my mind as we made our way home. I acted on instinct. Didn't want to leave him where he could be hurt again. Paxton told me Zeke was on his own. What if Chuck went to hurt him again after we left?

Showing my fangs to Chuck was another problem. I shouldn't have done it but again, instinct. Now I was home, where I should be relieved. Should be enjoying Paxton and us being alone.

"Theo?" Paxton's voice drew my attention to him. I was still sitting in the boat. The engine was off. The boat rocking ever so slightly.

"Sorry." I stood and grabbed as many bags as I could carry. I left Paxton on the boat with Zeke.

What did I tell Zeke now? I had to say something. Paxton had told me before he trusted him. This wasn't some little secret though. I brought him to my home. There was no going back. It wasn't like I could erase his thoughts.

They trailed behind me, bringing items we bought into the castle as well. I made sure to grab the blood. I didn't think Zeke would want to see that.

With the things in the boat finally put away, I went in search of Zeke and Paxton. I could hide, ignore them, which was the preferable choice, but that wouldn't get me anywhere. I also didn't want to leave it up to Paxton to tell Zeke everything.

I found them in the library, Zeke trailing his fingers over the spines of the books. I leaned against the doorway, watching them for a moment.

"I'm having a whole *Beauty and the Beast* moment here," Zeke said. I understood the reference but had never seen the movie that he would have.

Paxton smiled. "If only it were two stories with ladders, then it would rival the movie."

"It's not just the library, though this is great. You live in a castle in a remote location with a vampire."

"Yes, but he doesn't keep me here against my will and he's not a beast. He's a wonderful man."

"I still can't believe you live here."

"It was my father's," I said. Both of them turned my way. "He had it built many years ago to show off his wealth." I took a few steps into the room. "I've since made it more to my liking. This is one of my favorite rooms."

"This is Ostin Island then," Zeke said.

"Yes. I was brought here as a child by someone who worked for us. Pulled away from the death my family caused. The last I saw was the fire burning. I'd stayed here all this time, never leaving the island until Paxton came along. He's managed to coax me to leave and today was the first time I've set foot on the mainland in seventy years."

"Holy shit." Zeke's jaw dropped. "You've been here all this time, off the coast, and no one knew. Didn't they try looking for this place and said it was gone?"

Paxton nodded. "They did and found nothing. There's a cloaking spell over the island by the same mage we went to visit today. Novus doesn't know about Theo though. She provided the spell without that knowledge. In fact, you're the only other person alive who knows of Theo's existence. Well, people on land saw him and Chuck, but they don't know who he is."

"I implore you not to breathe a word of my name or what you've seen here when you return home," I said.

Zeke shook his head. "I would never. I understand how much trust you're putting in me. You're a king then?"

"When it comes to my family's fortune, I'm the royal heir. The head of the Ostin family. My father was that before me."

Paxton came over and took my hand in his. "You have me too."

"I do." I pressed a chaste kiss to his lips, wanting more, needing it, but didn't want to make Zeke feel uncomfortable.

"I still can't believe I'm standing in a castle on an island owned by an Ostin," Zeke murmured with wonder in his voice. "This is something out of dreams." He turned his head to look around the room and winced. It reminded me why he was here in the first place. Chuck put his hands on him.

I released Paxton's hand and went over to carefully tip Zeke's chin up. The mark was angrier than before. It would look worse before getting better. "I'm not a mage so I don't have the things to heal you," I told him. I wasn't going to offer him my blood. Paxton was special. Leven had been special too in a different way. It was a very big deal for me to offer my blood to a human. I knew other vampires did so without care. I wasn't them.

"It's just a bruise," he whispered. His hand came up to cover the skin. Tears welled in his eyes.

"You went through something traumatic. Someone put their hand around your neck with the intent to hurt you. I'm sorry for that."

"You didn't do it. You saved me."

"You're welcome to stay here for as long as you like. It's safe. No one will find you. We can return you home whenever you're ready."

Zeke looked over my shoulder toward Paxton then back at me. "Are you sure?"

"I wouldn't have offered if I wasn't. Besides, Pax likes you and he's a good judge of character. I trust you."

"That means a lot."

"How does lunch sound?" Paxton asked. "You can ask us any questions you have, which I'm sure are a lot. I couldn't believe what I was seeing the first time I came here."

Turning, I held Paxton's eyes. "I was awful to you that day."

"You were confused. Didn't know where the man you considered family was. I was standing in his place. I don't blame you for how you reacted."

"You deserved better."

"So did you."

Paxton was always trying to get me to see my worth. Without him, I'd probably never do that. I was slowly realizing I wasn't my family but that didn't erase the fear that I'd end up with the same fate as them. And now with another human on the island, I worried even more. What if I hurt him?

I must have squeezed my eyes shut because when I opened them, both Paxton and Zeke were standing before me.

Paxton looked at me but spoke to Zeke. "Theo worries about hurting us. He doesn't want to become his family. But I've told him many times that he isn't them. That he wouldn't kill me. With you here, it's not easy for him. Theo is a good man. He won't harm you."

"I'm not afraid of you, Theo," Zeke told me. "If anything, I'm grateful for what you did today. A man who wanted to kill me wouldn't have saved me from another. They never found out why your family did what they did, right?"

I shook my head, my throat becoming too tight to speak.

"Come on." Paxton reached for me, gave my hand a squeeze. "Let's find something to eat."

The three of us worked together to make a simple lunch of sandwiches and soup. We talked while we ate. Zeke asked questions. Paxton answered what he could and turned to me for others. By the time the food was gone, and the plates were cleaned, I felt more at ease.

Paxton was happy to have Zeke here, but he was never far from me as the day wore on. I was content to hold Paxton on the couch as they talked. I could see why Paxton liked Zeke. He was kind and caring.

It felt strange to have someone else in the castle. It was an adjustment when Paxton came. Now it felt like he was exactly where he belonged. Having Zeke here breathed more life into the place. What would it be like to have a big family within these walls? Sights and sounds of love? I'd never considered it before. Even once Paxton said he was staying. It was only him and me. But with Zeke it felt like this could be more. Could be a place where family came.

We were nearing time for bed. I saw Zeke's eyes drooping.

"Let's find you somewhere to sleep," Paxton said. "You have a lot of rooms to choose from. There's some on the other side of the castle if you want your privacy or others near us."

"Ummm... I..." Even if I couldn't hear the slight shake to his words, I could scent his fear.

"Zeke," I said his name firmly, but not harshly, to get his attention. "You don't have to stay on the other side of the castle or near us. The choice is yours, wherever you feel comfortable." I still worried about myself. It was that fear in the back of my mind that never left, waiting for something to snap in me and that blood craze to take over.

He let out a nervous laugh. "It's ridiculous, really. I'm a

grown man. I live on my own. There's no reason for me not to want to sleep in a room on the other side of the castle, but the thought of it has my stomach knotting and sweat breaking out all over. I really don't want to be alone over there. Why is that? I'm fine being alone at home but here it's different. Maybe it's that I was choked today, I'm not sure."

I gently gripped his biceps. He must have been at least eight inches shorter than me. "Zeke, focus on me. My voice." I was acutely aware of what it felt like to panic. Hell, I'd been doing it every time we got on that fucking boat.

His body shook against my hands. "I'm sorry," he said quietly.

"You don't have anything to be sorry for."

"You can sleep in my bed," Paxton offered. "I stay with Theo most nights anyway."

"Are you sure? I don't want to put you out."

"We can find you another bed near us if that's what you'd like. There's not much in the spare bedrooms. Not that mine is overly decorated but it feels more lived in. It's up to you."

"Yours please."

"Give me a few to change the sheets since I can't remember when the last time I did it was." He left up the stairs.

"Let's get you something to drink," I told him and led him to the kitchen. "When I first came here with Leven, the man who worked for my family and pulled me away when everything happened, he saw how upset I was. He was too. We lost everyone we loved." I reached into an upper cabinet and pulled out a small tin. Turning, I held it out to Zeke. "Open that and take a sniff." I realized how that sounded so I added quickly, "It's not drugs. I promise."

Zeke carefully opened it, revealing the cocoa powder inside. He dipped his head and inhaled. "What is that? I mean, I know it's chocolate, but it smells decadent."

"It was something my father bought for me when I was little. He stored it here. I remembered having it one time prior to when Leven and I arrived here on our own. Father told me he bought it from overseas on one of his trips. He knew I'd enjoy it."

"And it's lasted all this time? Seventy years and you've hardly drank it?"

"Just the once since we came back here. I couldn't bring myself to have it again. My memories of my parents were tainted after that day. I loved them but couldn't believe they did what they did. Killed those humans. It was hard for me to reconcile the people I loved with the monsters who murdered. Even now I struggle. But that cocoa soothed me that night. Reached some part deep inside and helped me relax enough to sleep. I'm not sure if it's still good now that I'm thinking about it. Might be best not to test that on you." This was a stupid idea.

He put the lid on the cocoa and handed it back to me with a small smile. "I'd rather not get sick from expired hot chocolate. But even if it was still good, I couldn't drink it. Not something that held those memories for you. That's why you hung on to it all this time, isn't it?"

I nodded, looking down at the tin with the embossed lid designed with a brand name on it. "I couldn't throw it out. I wanted to offer you a measure of comfort while you're here."

"Do you have tea?"

"I do." I went back to the cabinet and retrieved a box that held a variety of flavors. "Leven used to drink it at night. Pick which one you'd like, and I'll get the water started."

He did and then focused on the pendant around my neck. "What does it mean?"

I palmed the warm wood. "The O is for Ostin which I'm sure was easy to guess. The fire is because my family has the power of light and dark. We can create fire." I released the pendant and held open my palm where a flame appeared. I snuffed it out by closing my fist. "And we can create darkness through shadows, fog, etcetera." I let my magic come from me to fill the kitchen with shadows, taking the light out. It only lasted a second before I stopped it.

"And the wave?"

"My family has always lived near the ocean. Never ones to head inland. It was either along the coast or on islands. This isn't the first one we've inhabited." My family history went back far. I didn't think Zeke wanted to hear about it.

"It's interesting."

"It is."

That was where Paxton found us a few minutes later. In the kitchen making tea, talking about the good memories I had of my father.

23

PAXTON

Zeke had been with us for a few days. He told me this morning he would like to go back home. That he didn't want to keep hiding. I also thought he wanted to be comfortable in his own clothes. I washed his for him but in between he was wearing my clothes, which were a little too long and a little too tight on him. I was tall and slender. Zeke was shorter with a little more weight to him.

I loved having him here on the island with us. We stayed up late and played games. We talked. Well, Zeke and I did. Theo wasn't as chatty.

I was standing on the small pier leading to the boat in the center of the castle when Theo appeared. He was dressed in jeans that fit him just right. He had a black tank top on today that hugged his chest. Those muscular arms of his were on display. He didn't stop walking until he was chest to chest with me. Reaching up, he cupped the back of my neck and brought me in for a heated kiss. My knees went weak, but Theo was there with an arm around my waist to hold me up.

There was a sigh behind Theo. I broke our kiss to peer around him. Zeke had his head cocked slightly and was smiling. "I wish someone would kiss me like that. Not that I think I'll find it. I look nothing like you two."

My brow furrowed. "What are you talking about? You're very attractive."

He smacked his hand lightly on his stomach. "Sure. Everyone wants a guy with a soft middle."

Theo turned to face Zeke. "I'm not sure who told you that you weren't attractive, but you are. Plus, you're funny, kind, and a damn good cook."

A blush rose onto Zeke's cheeks. "You're sweet."

"No one has ever called me that before."

"Clearly, I'm not doing my job," I cut in and wrapped my arms around Theo's waist from behind.

He looked over his shoulder at me. "You take very good care of me." There was this look in his eyes that told me he was remembering just how well I treated him. Last night, I edged him then rode him until we both came and neither of us could see straight. We tried to be quiet and kept the windows closed until we slept. It was one of the times I was grateful for the stone walls separating the rooms.

Zeke let out another wistful sigh.

I grinned. "You ready to leave?"

"Yeah. I have bills to pay, which means back to driving people around." That was his only job, and he did it full time. It kept him in control and out in the world, not stuck in an office. Zeke was smart. Had to do everything on his own, much like I had. No one there to support either one of us. He had Theo and me now though.

"You could move here," Theo stated. His body tensed right after. It made me wonder if he thought about those words before saying them.

"What?" Zeke and I asked at the same time. Not that I'd mind having Zeke here. I'd love it. I was just surprised.

Theo shrugged. "We both like having you here. And I'm not sure you aren't in danger back on the mainland. You'd be safe with us."

Something had loosened in Theo the past few days with Zeke here. At first, he was scared he'd hurt him. As time passed, he relaxed. He wouldn't harm him. That was something I knew without a doubt. Theo wasn't a killer. Every encounter, every day, was proving it.

Zeke walked toward us and placed his hand on Theo's forearm. "While I greatly appreciate the offer, this is your home. Yours and Paxton's. I couldn't intrude. I have to get back to my life. But maybe I can vacation here when I get too stressed?"

"I don't think it's much of a getaway," Theo said. "But anytime you want to visit, get on the boat after the supply run. We can bring you here. I'm sorry we don't have a way for you to get a hold of us while we're here. I brought it up to Paxton to ask Novus, but he didn't think it was smart."

I shook my head. "There's something nice about being cut off from the world. If we introduced that back in, it takes away some of the magic of this place and I don't want to lose that. Though it would be good if you could get a hold of us if you needed to."

"I've made it this far in life, I'll be fine." Zeke smiled. That didn't mean I wouldn't worry. I'd see him again soon for the next supply run.

"Let's get going then."

We climbed onto the boat, and I used the magic within it so I could turn and talk to both Theo and Zeke while it moved. It wasn't long before we were pulling up to the pier at Sparkling. Theo was tense like I expected him to be. He looked to the parking lot, to the beach. Chuck didn't know when we'd get back. He'd have to sit here day in and day out to wait. He didn't have that kind of dedication. Sitting at his apartment to wait for me to come home was way easier.

I could see Zeke's car still in the parking lot from where we sat on the boat with the engine off so we could hear each other better. Zeke had a parking pass that allowed him to keep his car there. Something I didn't have when I owned mine. Not that I ever parked in this lot.

"Do you think we should have a car?" I asked Theo.

"Do you want one?"

"It might make things easier."

"What about me?" Zeke asked with a little pout. "If you have a car then you won't need me."

"That's not true," I told him. "You're our friend. We'd still see you."

Theo rested his hand over mine. "I think we should leave things as they are until Zeke is unable to help us when we're here."

"Okay."

I didn't like to depend on anyone throughout my life, yet that was what I was doing with Zeke. I could trust him. He wouldn't bail on me. But there was still this ingrained part of me that thought having a vehicle of ours we could park nearby would make things a lot easier. I couldn't leave it in the lot for weeks on end. There was a parking garage not far from here for the people who visited when the lot was full.

Zeke grinned. He wanted this. To feel like he was needed. It clicked how eager to please Zeke was. I couldn't believe I hadn't noticed it before. I always thought he was friendly, one of the nicest people I'd met. But maybe this was more than that. It could have been because of something in his past. There was a lot there I still didn't know about him and wouldn't pry.

"Thanks again," Zeke said. "Both of you. You're pretty much the only friends I have."

I leaned forward and hugged him. "We'll be back soon."

"Both of us," Theo added.

Zeke pulled back and looked at Theo. "Are you okay?"

"I don't like being here with people watching me." I glanced around and didn't see anyone paying us any mind. "I wanted to make sure you were safe though. There's no way I want Pax coming here alone again." I'd argue and say I could take care of myself, but the truth was, I'd fought Chuck many times. I didn't always get away and had no desire to fight him again. With Theo there, Chuck wouldn't come near me.

Zeke stood. "You're a good friend, Theo. Someone I'm glad is on my side. I'll see you both soon." He got off the boat and made his way toward the parking lot.

Theo and I stayed where we were, watching him to make sure everything was okay. Zeke put on a good front. Tried to make it seem like he was all right. The tremble in his voice said he wasn't. I knew better than to press. Zeke wanted to go home. Work. We'd support that.

"Why'd he stop?" I asked when Zeke got to his car and stared at the side of it. He lifted his hands to his face and stepped back, still looking down. "Something's not right." I was up and moving without another word.

Theo's steps thundered behind mine up the gangway, down the pier, and into the parking lot. I faltered when I saw the car. The tires were slashed, completely flattened. There were long lines etched down the side of the car. I was surprised it hadn't been towed yet. But that would mean someone here actually cared about another person's property. They were too shallow for that. Too engrossed in their own lives.

"Chuck did this," I said. I didn't have a doubt in my mind. That asshole would have been pissed he had to tuck tail and run. He came back when everyone was gone and got his revenge.

"Are you sure?" Theo asked.

"Yeah, it's the kind of petty shit he'd pull. Since we were gone, there was no other way to get revenge."

"Pull up that app on your phone and order us a car to take us to your old building."

"No way. We're not going there to confront him." My stomach churned at the thought. That was the last place I wanted to be. Where so much happened to me. Where no matter what I never felt truly safe.

"I won't let anything happen to you."

"I don't want to go," I whispered.

"Stay here with Zeke. Let me handle it." I had a feeling his way of doing so would be killing Chuck, and I couldn't let that happen as much as I'd love to rid him from the world. Theo wasn't a murderer. Bail money wasn't something I wanted to arrange.

"You're not going to go back to the boat, are you?" I asked.

"Not before handling this. Zeke needs to feel safe. I want to ensure he does."

"Fuck," I muttered. If Theo could face his hell and come onto land, I could head back to my apartment building. We could be a disaster together. Although, right now, Theo looked nothing like the man who was scared to step foot in this town. He was determined, ready to handle Chuck. I had to be there to rein him in.

I opened the app on my phone and ordered a car. "Five minutes." They were usually easy to get here. After all, money talked and those who came to Sparkling had plenty of it.

"We'll take care of your car after," Theo said to Zeke. "I'll pay for the damages."

"You don't have to do that."

"Let him," I interjected. "He has the money, and he hardly spends it. Besides, I don't think he'll settle unless he knows you're taken care of." If I was a jealous man I'd wonder if Theo had feelings for Zeke, but I knew better. Theo only looked at me with desire. He cared about Zeke, sure. Not in the same way he did me.

The SUV pulled up and parked in the lot.

"Do you want to stay here?" I asked Zeke. Bringing him face-to-face with the man who bruised his neck and fucked up his car wouldn't be easy for him.

"No. I'll come but I'll wait outside."

"That works." It also kept the violence away from Zeke. I'd be damned if I sat in the car too though.

24

THEO

The thought of Paxton living here, scared for his well-being night after night had me wanting to punch things. I'd hold it in and wait to see Chuck. He'd be a good thing to take my anger out on.

Zeke stayed in the car with the driver, who seemed like a decent guy. He had a nice vehicle and didn't look anywhere close to being a threat. Nevertheless, Zeke had Paxton's phone number and said he'd call if there were any issues.

Paxton and I made our way into the building and up the stairs to the second floor. I had my hat on and sunglasses in place. He told me Chuck would hear us coming, no matter how quiet we were. I wanted him to hear me. Hear who was coming for him.

We walked down the hall where Paxton pointed to Chuck's door. It opened when we were a few feet away. The scent of rotten garbage leaked out from the room. Chuck's hair was slicked back. His tank top had stains in the pits. He sneered at us, his teeth rotten. This man was a disgusting waste of space.

"Well, well, well," he said. We stopped a foot from him, I kept Paxton behind me. If this asshole wanted to get him, he had to go through me first. "If it isn't the vampire who threatened my life. Did you come here to finish the job?" Why was he so cocky? This was nothing like the man I met the last time who pissed himself and scurried away like the rat he was.

I widened my stance. My boots sat heavy on my feet. I hadn't planned on kicking the shit out of anyone today, but I wore them anyway. They weren't meant for running. That was the last thing I'd do. "I want reparation for the damage you've done to my friend's car."

"I don't know what you're talking about."

"Very well." I reached forward, grabbing his shirt in my fist. The scent of him nearly drove me away. "How many teeth do you have left? I wonder how it would feel to swallow them."

His hand shot up but not to hit it. He was holding a newspaper I hadn't noticed. "Don't read the paper wherever you crawled off to? You should. You're front-page news."

Paxton stepped forward to rip it from Chuck's hand.

"Paxy, you missed me, didn't you? Couldn't get enough of my cock?"

I didn't think. I punched him in the nose then brought my knee up to nail his balls. He was lucky I didn't rip them clean off his body. He bent over as he cried out. I swept my leg around and took his feet out from under him, so he landed flat on the ground, his face meeting it.

The door to my left opened. An older woman with curly gray hair peeked her head out. She gasped when she saw Chuck on the ground.

"He slipped," I told her.

She looked up at me. "It appears so."

"Fuck you, you crazy old bitch!" Chuck yelled.

My boot planted on the back of his neck, holding him to the ground. "Apologize to her."

"Go to hell!"

I pressed harder, this time digging my heel into his cheek.

"Fine, I'm sorry, you nosy old bag!"

I brought my foot back and kicked him in the ribs. He cried out again. "I don't know how he keeps falling," I said to the older woman, my face showing no emotion.

"It's a mystery," she replied then ducked back into her apartment. I heard the door lock. She must have run into Chuck one too many times. I felt sorry for her and everyone else here who had to deal with him.

"Theo..." Paxton whispered.

"Not now. I have to teach this asshole a lesson."

"No, Theo, you need to see this." He held the paper out to me with a shaking hand.

I took it and looked at the front page. My stomach sank. It was like all the blood was draining from my body.

Ostin Heir Alive, read the headline.

There was no recent picture with the article but there was one of the fire that day. The buildings burning. Seeing it transported me back in time. I could still smell the blood in the air. The scent of gasoline as it was being poured. I felt the lick of the flames. Heard the screams from my family as they were being staked right in front of me.

I stumbled back, hitting a wall. My eyes burned with tears. No, not my family. Not my parents.

I cried and reached for them as Leven dragged me away. I wanted him to go back so we could try and save them.

"Theo." I knew that voice. It didn't belong in my nightmare though.

How did everything go so wrong? My family wouldn't have done this, yet I saw it with my own eyes. They weren't the people I loved and looked up to. I couldn't stop them, so I hid like a coward until Leven found me.

"Theo."

"No, please," I whispered.

I was being shaken. "Theo!"

The scene faded away, leaving a man I loved but didn't deserve in front of me.

He searched my face with worry evident on his. "We have to get out of here."

I blinked and let him pull me away. There was something in my hand that I couldn't release. We went down a flight of stairs, out a door, into a vehicle, and started moving. I wasn't sure what was going on and didn't care.

"What happened?" another voice asked. Zeke.

"Theo, you have to look at me." I did. Paxton was so damn beautiful. So much better than me.

"I'm sorry," I choked out.

He cupped my cheeks. "You have nothing to be sorry for. I'm going to get you home, okay?"

I nodded as tears fell. How could something that happened decades ago be so fresh in my mind? I thought I was past this. No longer tortured by my memories.

Zeke and Paxton talked while I focused on the pain residing in my chest. The loss of the ones I loved. How could I still love them when they did such horrible things that night?

We stopped. A door opened.

"Theo, we have to get Zeke inside. I want to make sure his apartment hasn't been broken into." His words were enough to snap me out of my hell. This instinct to protect the people I cared about rose to the surface.

I slid out of the vehicle. My arms and legs felt like they were filled with lead. Every step took a monumental effort. But I went. For Zeke. For Paxton.

Zeke's apartment building didn't look much better than Paxton's. He was on the third floor. Luckily, there was no neighbor to torture him.

"I'm sorry the place isn't so great," Zeke said. "But it's safe. I don't have to worry here."

"It's fine." Paxton was talking to him. "I don't judge."

We got to the door. Zeke unlocked it and the three of us went inside. I stayed by the door while they looked through the space.

Zeke peeked around a corner. "Everything is where it's supposed to be."

"Good, I'm glad. Are you going to be okay here?"

"Yeah, I'll be fine."

I turned to Paxton. "The money."

"Oh, right." Paxton took his wallet out, retrieving five hundred dollars. He always kept money on him just in case, although he did worry about being robbed. "Take this. It's all I have on me. I can meet you tomorrow to pay the rest for your car."

"I don't want your money. I have enough to cover it." By the sound of his voice, he didn't.

"I won't sleep well unless I know you're taken care of." Paxton extended his arm. Zeke hesitantly took the money. "Get an estimate for the paint. Get the tires replaced. We'll write a check for the paint and pay you back whatever else is owed for the tires."

"It's too much."

"Zeke, I know how hard it is to take money from someone. But this isn't because we feel sorry for you. If it weren't for me, none of this would have happened. I want to make things right."

Zeke sighed. "Fine, but I'm not happy about it."

"I get it."

The money traded hands and we said our goodbyes. I didn't move from the hallway until I heard the locks engage on the door.

"What's he going to do about his job?" I asked.

"The tires shouldn't take long to be replaced. He can drive the car then. It's not ideal. The scratches are huge but at least Chuck didn't write anything into the paint. When using those apps to request rides, the most important things are the timeliness of the driver, the cleanliness of the car interior, and how polite the driver is."

I nodded. We'd cover his bills. All of them. I wasn't letting Zeke try to find a way to handle things or use his savings, however much of it he had. We'd pay him back. Every bit of it.

The vehicle was waiting for us. We got inside and started the drive back to the pier. Paxton thanked the man, and we made the walk down to the boat.

"He figured it out," I murmured before Paxton got the engine started. "How?"

"You showed him your fangs but that could have been any vampire. Granted, we are in Delaware. This is where you're from." He paused while I thought back to that day when I had Chuck pinned to the side of Zeke's car. What tipped him off?

"Theo?"

"Yeah?"

"Your pendant is showing."

I glanced down. I kept it on a leather cord around my neck. "It must have come out when I was in your old building."

"The same had to have happened the other day. There's no other way he'd know. My guess is he went on the internet, typed in vampire and the symbol on your pendant, and your family appeared in the results." He pulled his phone out of his pocket. His fingers went fast over the screen then he turned it so I could see. There it was. Article after article about the Ostin family and our crest.

The paper crinkled in my hand when I balled it into a fist. I was still holding on to it. Paxton carefully pried my fingers away to take it from me. He looked it over, but I couldn't bear to see it again, so I glanced out at the water.

"It's a tabloid," he said. "A shit paper. People only read these for make-believe gossip. I doubt anyone will take it seriously."

"It's enough to get people talking."

"Maybe."

"I'm the last surviving member of my family. If they think there's a drop of truth to it, they're going to dig. I'm sorry I dragged you into this, Pax. This is a nightmare, and you shouldn't be wrapped up in it. You should pack your things when we get back. Find a new place to live far from here. I'll give you more money. Enough to buy a big house with the best security system. Whatever you need."

"Theo, stop."

"You could live a full life. Have everything you've ever wanted. I don't need the money. Take it all. As long as you're happy, that's all that matters."

Paxton leaned forward and pressed his lips to mine, effectively stopping me from saying anything else. He didn't relent until he was able to get me to respond and kiss him back. The kiss heated up fast and died down just as quickly.

Paxton pecked my lips a few times before putting a couple of inches between us. "I'm not going anywhere. Not for all the money in the world. You're stuck with me. I don't care what they say about you. They don't know you like I do. There is nothing they can print to make me stop loving you."

"Pax..." Goddammit the tears were back in my eyes. I didn't want him to leave. But I had to give him the option. It would be the easiest path for him. The one where he wouldn't be talked about for being with me.

He reached up to grip the back of my neck. "You and me against everyone else. Fuck them. They haven't lived your life. They haven't seen what you've gone through."

"They're judging me." The paper said so. Already made speculations about what I'd be like.

"No matter where we go in this life, there will always be someone waiting to criticize us. Someone who hates how we look, talk, dress. Who we love. They. Don't. Matter. None of them." His other hand pressed against my chest over my heart. It was beating rapidly beneath his palm. "I love you, Theo Ostin."

"I love you too."

"Good, then let's go home. We need to talk about how you thought I'd just leave you and take your money. That shit isn't ever happening."

I couldn't help the spark of hope that flared in my chest. Paxton had seen me at my worst. Broken, afraid, panicked, so many things. And he stayed even when I tried to push him away.

25

PAXTON

As soon as we were home and I had the boat docked, I took Theo's hand in mine and dragged him into the castle, up the stairs, and to his bedroom. He didn't say a word, which I appreciated because I was angry. I loved him but if he thought he was going to try to shove me away from him, thinking it was for the best, we were going to have words.

"In the shower," I told him. "I want you clean. No trace of Chuck's blood on you."

Theo looked down, noticing the tiny droplets on his hand. It wasn't much but enough that I wasn't doing anything with him like that.

He stripped his clothes off and dropped them into the hamper then disappeared into the bathroom while I paced the floor. Today was awful. There wasn't any way to sugarcoat it. Chuck was a raging piece of shit, like always. I did love watching Theo put him to the ground. Mrs. Alberts didn't even notice me. Then again, she and I didn't have lengthy conversations. I was usually trying to get into my apartment as fast as I could to avoid a confrontation with Chuck or one of his friends.

I went over to the windows and opened them both up,

letting the salty air in. I stood there, taking deep breaths and letting them out, trying to calm myself. Theo would shut down and blame himself if I showed him how much he upset me. I had to tell him, show him, I was in this for the long haul.

The fresh air felt good. I tried doing this while we were on the boat, but I was too worked up. Now that we were safe, no one to see us, I could slow things down. Breathe. Let go of some of the tension in my body.

"Pax?"

I turned to find Theo watching me with a towel slung low on his hips. Water droplets ran in rivulets down his chest over every ridge and dip of his abs. He was a work of art.

Stepping forward, I closed the distance between us and focused on the pendant around his neck. I traced the edge of it with my finger.

"I'm—"

"Don't say it. I don't regret anything, Theo. And this pendant... It's probably the reason Chuck figured out who you are." My eyes met his. "That crest, the same one I wear around my neck, it brought me to you. I could never wish that didn't happen. Don't you know how much you mean to me? I tell you I love you but it's deeper than that. You're a part of my soul. You can say how I'd be better off without you. How I wouldn't have to deal with any of this if you weren't in my life. The words would be empty because I can't go back. I don't want to. You're the best thing that's ever happened to me. I don't care what the world throws at us. I'll stay by your side, supporting you, loving you for as long as we both live. Do you understand what I'm saying?"

His eyes, fuck, they did me in. Tears gathered in them, little pools of emotion. Theo was so much more than the heir to the Ostin fortune. The king of his family. It was the complete person who I loved. I didn't care about his title or his money. I lived my life without any and could live the rest the same. It was Theo I wanted.

"I want to marry you, Theo Ostin," I whispered. "I want to show the world you're mine. Do you want that? Do you want me forever?"

"Pax, do you realize what you're saying?"

"I'm asking you to marry me. It doesn't have to be anytime soon. I want you to know I'm not going anywhere. Ever. I will never love someone else like I love you. What do you say? Marry me?"

One solitary tear trickled down his cheek. "My heart is yours, Paxton Huxley. Wherever you go, whatever you do, I'll be with you. I'll overcome anything I need to, so you know just how much I love you. I'll marry you. But there's something else I need to ask you."

"Anything."

"I don't think I can ever let you go. Every day you age, slower now that you're drinking my blood. But it's not forever."

"You want me to become a vampire."

He nodded. "It's a lot to ask. It will change you. You'll be just like me."

"Being like you isn't a bad thing."

"I could snap. Go into a blood craze. But if you're a vampire, I can't kill you by drinking from you."

"Theo, you would never kill me." Being a vampire, that was a lot. Yet, as I stood here with the man I loved more than anything before me, with his heart bleeding through his voice, there was nothing I could deny him. And who was I kidding? There weren't enough years for me to love him. I wanted an infinite amount. I wanted to wake up every day and know I would be with him for the rest of time. Becoming like him was something I desired too.

"You don't have to tell me now."

"Yes."

"You should think about it. Make sure you're positive it's what you want."

"Like you thought about marrying me?"

"Loving you is as simple as breathing. My heart beats for you."

"As mine does for you." I took a deep breath and let it out. "I'm not ready to get turned today though."

"I won't rush you. We can do it whenever you want."

"Vampire first then a wedding?"

"Yes."

I grinned. "Do you know how happy you make me?"

"Even with everyone finding out the truth about me? That I'm alive? They'll know you're with me, Pax. It won't be easy going to the mainland."

"I never cared what people thought about me before. Why would I start now?"

"I'm not letting you go there alone."

"I didn't think you would."

He squeezed his eyes shut. "I'm scared."

"I know, but I'm here. I'll be with you every step of the way. You got thrown into the thick of things. I finally get you back there and everything crashes down around us."

His lids lifted slowly. "Last chance to back out. I won't let you go after this. I won't be able to."

"No more pushing me away."

"No."

"I'm yours."

I gave in and reached for him, put my hands on his hips and pressed our bodies together. Enough talking. I said everything I needed to. Hell, I proposed to him. Even I didn't see that coming. It felt right though. Perfect. I didn't regret it, not for a second. Theo was going to be mine in every sense of the word. And if other people didn't like it, they could go to hell.

I brushed my lips over his. "I want to make love to you."

He moaned. "I need you in me, Pax. Take me. Claim me."

Reaching down, I pulled the towel from his body and dropped it on the floor. I backed him toward the bed until his legs bumped it and he sat down.

"On your back for me," I told him. "Hold your legs up and show yourself to me."

Theo moved quickly and got into position, no questions asked. Here was this vampire, so fucking powerful, yet he let me see him like this. Yielded to me. He showed me every part of himself inside and out. It was amazing and made me feel powerful in return.

I shed my clothes, grabbed the lube from the nightstand, and crawled over top of him, not wasting time. I coated my fingers and started stretching him. Theo reacted beautifully. He gave me his moans and his hole. I pushed one finger in, stroked it over his prostate. Theo needed to get out of his head. This was one of the few ways I could guarantee he did so.

"Pax, fuck!" he called out as I kept a steady rhythm. Precum leaked from his tip, falling onto his stomach.

Taking pity on him, I pulled back to add another finger, moving them around, stretching him more before I added a third. Theo took them without complaint. It burned; it had to. But he wanted this as badly as I did him. That little bit of pain would give way to pure pleasure soon.

The room was quiet as I flipped the lid open on the lube again. The cool liquid hit my dick and I let out a hiss. I threw the lube down on the bed, not caring where it landed so I could take my dick into my hand and thoroughly coat it.

"God, Theo, I'm so hard for you."

He whimpered; his legs still held up to his chest.

I leaned over and tapped my dick against his hole. My lips hovered over his. "You ready for me?"

"Please."

The feeling of his body around my tip was nothing I could explain. It was the best sensation. Had my back bowing, my mind checking out, and a moan tearing up my throat. I couldn't stop to give him time to adjust. I had to be buried deep inside.

When I finally was, I leaned down to blanket him with my body. My lips met his in a punishing kiss. Our tongues battled for dominance at first as Theo's legs wrapped around my waist. But eventually he gave in. I wanted him to let go, and he was.

My hips started moving on their own. It wasn't a conscious thought. It was like I couldn't get close enough. I reached down and took his ass in one hand to hold him while I pounded into him. No matter what I did, it wasn't enough.

"Theo, I need..."

"What? Tell me and it's yours."

I fucked him harder, faster, chasing what felt far out of reach. "I don't know. Shit. I need more."

Theo removed his legs from me. I slid from his body. He rolled us over, so I was on my back, and he was over me. His lips were parted, fangs out, eyes nothing but dark orbs. He straddled my waist then gripped my dick so he could lower down over me. Every inch he covered was in slow motion.

"You feel amazing," I rasped.

His powerful legs flexed as he shuttled his body up and down, doing all the work. His dick was hard and angry-looking between us, begging for attention. I couldn't believe I kept my hands off it this long.

Reaching forward, I wrapped him up with my hand and started stroking him. This was what I needed. The sight before me. The man I loved riding my dick while showing me his true self.

It made me wonder what it was going to be like when he finally drank from me. When I got to drink from him. I'd read it was a painful experience to be changed but didn't last long before euphoria took over. Sex and drinking went hand in hand, and fuck did I want that.

Theo brought his wrist to his mouth and sliced it open. I quickly took it in my free hand and pulled it to my lips, needing the taste of him on my tongue. I sucked. He came with a shout. Cum splashed on my stomach and chest. In my next breath, I was emptying inside of him. Coming so hard I thought I was going to black out. It went on and on until Theo folded forward to lick his blood from my lips.

Holy shit, I wouldn't tire of this. Theo was everything. His blood flowed through my body. His cum painted my skin. And his name was the only one I'd call out when I came.

He was mine. Fucking hell, he was my fiancé.

26

THEO

Paxton was nearly vibrating in his seat. The urge to get to Zeke and check on him was strong. Paxton even took the boat out twice since we'd been back so he could get a signal and look for messages. There were none. We both hoped that was a good thing and Zeke was fine. Or maybe he knew he couldn't contact us and didn't try. I kept that thought to myself.

We were on our way for another supply run. I was nervous but not like in times past. This was about me being afraid of everyone knowing who I was. That I was the man being spoken about in the paper. By now I wondered how many other news outlets picked up on it. Whether they discounted it as tabloid bullshit or gave it some merit.

The first thing we noticed when we had the boat docked and were off it was Zeke leaning against his car in the parking lot. His head was bent down, his profile to us, as he looked at his phone. His head lifted as we approached, a smile on his lips but that wasn't what I was focused on. No, it was the bruise on his face that was no longer black since it wasn't fresh. It was a horrid yellow color.

I strode toward him, not stopping until I had his chin in my hand so I could tilt his head to get a better look. Once I removed his sunglasses, anger swelled in me. There was no doubt in my mind who did this.

"I knew putting on sunglasses wouldn't work," he said. "You'd wonder why I kept them on. I'd have to show you. This way, it's like ripping off a bandage. You've seen it. Can we go now?"

"Zeke," Paxton whispered. "When did this happen?"

"Does it matter? He hit me. Didn't like that I had the money to replace my tires. Saw me here when I was enjoying the weather, looking out from the end of the pier. I got back and found him waiting by my car. He hit me, threatened me, and fled." He shrugged.

There were a lot of questions I wanted to ask. What came out was, "Why were you on the pier?" From what Paxton had told me, Zeke preferred to stay close to home unless he was driving. It was more of a comfort zone for him.

Zeke ducked his head. "I missed you two, your home. I was being stupid."

"No, you weren't," Paxton stated. "We missed you too. Both of us." He was right. I enjoyed having Zeke around.

He brushed right over Paxton's comment. "Let's go get what you need."

"Not until you agree to move in with us," I cut in. I didn't need to check with Paxton to know he'd want this too.

"What?" Zeke's eyes went wide.

Paxton grinned. "You heard him. What do you say?"

"I thought when you asked last time it was a joke. How would we do this?"

"We can work it out later," I added. "What's important is keeping you safe."

He sniffled and looked around. "I'd been thinking about my life here since we last saw each other. Wondering why I stayed.

Why I kept fighting when it felt like I was barely treading water. I'm not happy. At least, not on my own."

Paxton took Zeke's hand in his. "You're our friend. We want you to come stay with us. Just don't get any ideas about Theo." He winked. Paxton wasn't as possessive of me as I was of him. I still liked it when he said things like that though.

"I don't know what to say."

"Yes would be beneficial," I replied.

"Yes."

I nodded. "It's settled."

We spent the next hour packing up the belongings Zeke wanted to take with him. He had other things he wanted to keep so Paxton arranged for movers and a storage unit to put everything in. We'd do that on the next supply run. It was too much for today and people weren't available to do it that quickly unless we paid them more, which I was happy to do, but Zeke insisted against that.

With the car full of his belongings, still leaving room for supplies and us, we went and ran the rest of our errands. The grocery store required more time since we were buying for the three of us now. We always had extra food at home in case we couldn't get here in time, but we needed to stock up more now.

The entire time we were in the store, I felt like everyone was watching me. I had my hat brim pulled low. The sunglasses were off. Paxton kept shopping and I stayed near him. It didn't take long before we were in front of the cashier, paying for our food.

We loaded the car up and got out of there. I was shaking when we got back to the pier. My shirt was sticking to me from sweat. Zeke looked nervous as well. I must have been affecting him. I hated that I couldn't reassure him. I was too busy trying to keep myself from falling apart. Paxton kept it together for all of us.

Zeke parked in the lot by the pier, made sure to hang the sign in his car saying he was able to park longer though we'd need to come back and move his car, so they didn't tow it after a week of going nowhere. But right now, we had to leave.

With our arms full, we started walking toward the boat. We would need to make more than one trip.

A few feet from the pier, a loud explosion wrenched through the air. I dropped the bags I was holding and pulled Paxton to me, turned us around, and covered his body with mine as I pushed him to the ground.

Around us people were screaming, running away. We had to get up or we were going to be trampled. I helped Paxton to his feet and then Zeke. I felt like shit for not shielding him as well. My first thought was Paxton and keeping him safe.

We glanced back to the boat and saw flames on what was left of it. Pieces of wood were scattered in the water and on the pier. There was only one man I could think of who would want to hurt us like this.

"Let's go," I said as I scooped up the bags along with their contents and put them back into the car. We had no way back to the island, but I was above caring about that right now. Chuck needed to be dealt with.

"Where are we going?" Zeke asked once we were in the car.

Paxton sighed. There would be no talking me out of this, and he knew it. "To Chuck's. I get it, Theo. I really do. But confronting him won't solve anything. We could drive farther up the coast, rent a boat, get the hell out of here."

"I won't stand by while he gets away with this. We could have been on that boat, Paxton. We could have been killed. You could have been..." The thought was like ice being poured through my veins. Losing my parents was awful. Losing Paxton would destroy me.

"What about the police?" Zeke asked.

"They won't listen to a vampire whose family murdered a town of people," I said. "Once they figured out who I was, they'd probably lock me up thinking I blew up my own boat and charge me with endangering humans."

"I didn't think about that."

"The world won't see me as you do. They'll go by what they've read, heard. Let's go see Chuck and find a boat to rent." I was done with this fucking land. I wanted off it. Back to my castle. Back to the place I sought solace. It was once a prison. With Paxton, it was a home.

We parked a couple of blocks from the apartment building and approached it from the back. There was a door there that Paxton said was never locked. It was a rear entrance to the small and shitty lobby where no one ever sat behind the desk. The tenants fended for themselves.

Inside, we came to a halt. As did the conversation between the people in the room. And there were a lot of them. Cameras. Microphones. People in suits. And standing in the middle of them was Chuck with a grin. I didn't miss the stake in his hand. The one made from the same trees that were used to kill my family. He knew damn well what he was doing when he let me see it.

He blew up our boat knowing it would drive us here. I started weighing the options of killing him in front of everyone. The only thing stopping me was Paxton. I couldn't go to prison and leave him alone. Nor did I want to be apart from him.

"Mr. Ostin!" was shouted by multiple reporters.

"Are you the only surviving member of your family?"

"Have you felt a blood craze and gone after anyone?"

"Where do you live?"

"Was that your boat that blew up at the pier?"

"Did you have anything to do with that?"

My mind spun as we became encircled by the reporters. I

looked from left to right. Tried to find a way out. My heart was about to pound out of my chest. Paxton was clutching my arm. Questions were being slung his way too. Zeke stood pressed to my other side.

"Paxton Huxley, who is Mr. Ostin to you?"

"Are you together?"

"Do you live with him?"

"Are you under a spell?"

"Has he tried to turn you?"

There were people vying for Zeke's attention too. They didn't know who he was, but they were still pressing him for answers. He had his eyes squeezed shut and his arms wrapped around his stomach.

That was enough of this. We had to get out of here. I didn't care who I shoved down in the process.

I took Zeke's arm while Paxton still held on to my other one and started pushing through. Darkness descended around us as I let my magic flow from me. It became black as night, but I knew where I had to go. Paxton and Zeke were quick to keep up. I was grateful I could no longer see the cameras being shoved in our faces. Too bad I couldn't rip them from their hands and shove them down their fucking throats. Vultures. All of them.

We finally made it back to the door we came in through and pushed outside. I kept the darkness cloaking us and tried to shut the door, but the sea of reporters wouldn't let me. We turned and rushed around the side of the building. Before I knew what was happening, someone grabbed the front of my shirt and started pulling me forward. I let the thick shadows stay behind us as I took in an SUV with darkened windows.

"Get in," the man said.

I jerked away and released Paxton and Zeke, ready to fight this man. But then he turned to me.

Dark eyes. Hair slightly lighter than mine. Scruff that was trimmed close to his face. But it was what was hanging from his wrist when he raised his hand to fend me off that had me pausing. A pendant. Identical to mine.

I met his eyes again, studying him. Everything faded away but him. "Where did you get that?" I asked.

"You want to have a fucking reunion right now? Get in the car, Theo!"

Paxton was urging me forward. It was either get in with a man who I didn't know, wearing a bracelet with my family's crest on it, or face the reporters. The man won.

Paxton, Zeke, and I piled in and shut the doors while the man jumped behind the wheel and drove as fast as he could. He made sharp turns down the blocks. None of us spoke until he stopped the vehicle along a street where there was nothing but an abandoned warehouse and a few cars on cinder blocks.

He turned around to face the three of us in the back seat and grinned. "Hello, Cousin."

Most people would probably be in shock. Not me. My eyes narrowed while I tried to figure out what he was playing at.

"You don't believe me?" he asked. "Okay. Let me paint a little picture for you. Seventy-three years ago. Young Theo was playing in his room with his cousin. They sat in the middle of the floor as a train set went around them. Theo was enamored by the train, but his cousin was much more interested in the model plane he had built that morning."

Disbelief swam in me. This couldn't be my cousin. But no one else would know that. I remembered that day. Remembered how excited I was about the train. "What color was the plane?"

"Red, of course."

"Arbor?"

"In the flesh. Now, if we're done here, I think we should get the fuck off the street and into hiding. Nice to see you again, Paxton."

I swung my gaze to Paxton's. He was staring at Arbor, eyes so big I thought they were going to fall out of his head.

"How do you know my cousin?" I asked.

"He's... His name isn't Arbor."

"Well, it is," Arbor said. "But you knew me as Mitchell."

"What the hell is going on here?" I yelled.

"We dated," Paxton whispered.

My eyes blazed with anger as my arm shot out to grip Arbor by the throat.

Paxton was yelling, tugging on my arm. "He didn't do anything to me, Theo. He wasn't the one who hurt me. He was actually nice."

"Nice?" I seethed. "Did you touch my fiancé, Arbor?" I was ready to tear his head from his shoulders.

Paxton hit my arm. "Theo, seriously! Let him go!"

"I never hurt him," Arbor rasped out. He could pull me off. He was as strong as I was, but he wasn't fighting me, which made me realize they were both telling the truth.

I released him with a shove. He started rubbing his throat.

"Can we save the macho bullshit for when we're home?" Paxton asked. "We need to go."

Arbor turned back around and got us moving again. With Paxton's direction, he drove us back to Zeke's car, who hadn't said a word since we got in Arbor's vehicle. We got out, leaving Arbor alone in his SUV, and followed behind him down to a marina where he had a boat. It was time to go home and figure out what the hell was going on.

27

PAXTON

Holy motherfucking shit. The man I dated briefly, the one who actually treated me with respect, the man who all we did was kiss, was Theo's fucking cousin.

We drove to the marina in silence. It was south along the Maryland coast. Luckily, there was no one following us. The tension in the car remained high. Theo sat up front so he could stretch his legs out. I was in the back with the stuff we bought, grateful Zeke brought coolers for me. That was something he started doing when he was driving me regularly. I appreciated it.

Arbor pulled into a lot, and we followed, parking alongside him.

"We'll come back for your car," Theo said.

Zeke nodded.

"Are you sure you want to come with us?"

"I do. This is just... a lot."

"It is and I'm sorry about that."

"Theo, it's not your fault. You got us out of there. Kept us safe. You have nothing to apologize for."

Theo didn't need to say anything else for me to know he'd

let this weigh him down. He didn't like putting Zeke or me in the public's eye with who he was. By association, they'd make guesses about us as well. They didn't know us, only thought they did. I still felt the worst for Theo. People would make assumptions that he was like his parents. That was clear by the questions being thrown his way and the stake Chuck was holding. I wished I could go back there and drive it through Chuck's chest.

We got out of the car, each grabbing bags, and Arbor showed us to his boat. It wasn't anything huge, but it was big enough that it had a bedroom and bathroom inside. The good thing was that it looked like it would fit into the island.

"Have you been living on this?" Theo asked.

"Yeah, I liked to be able to get away. If I rented or bought something on land, it would be too easy to track me."

"No one knew who you were?"

"No, I told everyone my name was Mitchell Martinson. I have fake IDs and all. Money talks and got me what I needed." If Theo had access to all his parents' money, I was guessing Arbor did too but...

"How did you get your parents' money if everyone thought you were dead?" I asked Theo.

"Mage spells. You'd be surprised what things they can do. Technology is easily manipulated. Before a computer was used for everything, Leven would use spells to make the people at the bank forget when he transferred money from my parents' or my account into his. Since he was the one handling everything, he had access to all the money. My father trusted him, so I did the same."

"And now? Can you claim their money since you're alive and everyone knows?"

"Yes, I suppose I can. Though I have such a vast amount in mine, I won't need to touch theirs for quite some time." I knew

Theo had money, but now I was really curious just how much. Not that it mattered. We could live the rest of our days in the castle, doing nothing but enjoying our time together, and I'd be more than happy.

Arbor clapped his hands together. "Can we get a move on? I really don't like being out here exposed to everyone at the moment."

"Right," Theo said.

We got moving again and unloaded everything from Zeke's car onto the boat.

As we were getting situated to go out to sea, Arbor turned to Zeke. "We haven't met." He offered his hand. "Arbor Ostin."

"Zeke Wallingford." He took Arbor's hand.

Arbor grinned and a blush rose up Zeke's cheeks.

It didn't take long before we were on our way out of the marina and toward the island. Theo sat beside me, his arm around my shoulders. I leaned into him. It was a hell of a day. The boat blew up which we'd have to replace. I saw Arbor, who revealed himself as Theo's cousin. Everyone knew who Theo was now. That Zeke and I knew him as well. And Arbor was in the mix. I wasn't sure if anyone saw him or not, thanks to the darkness Theo threw over us.

Arbor's long whistle brought my head up. The castle was in front of us.

"I didn't know this place still existed," he said. "I read it was gone. No one could find it."

"Leven had it cloaked, and I threw enough fog around it to help. Our family pendant allows us to see and access it."

Arbor slowed the boat and turned around to face us. "So, you're the reason the sea at Desolate Beach looks the way it does?"

"Yes."

"I always thought it was an aftereffect of everything that

happened. If I had known this was still here, that you were still alive, I would have come."

"You never tried to search for the island?" I asked.

"No, didn't see the point. No one had found it."

"And this whole time you lived on a boat that could have easily brought you to it thanks to your bracelet."

"I didn't know it could, but also, I never used to wear this." He shook his wrist. The pendant was on a braided, brown leather cord. "I kept it in safekeeping on the boat. I only put it on today to show Theo, so he'd know who I was."

"You lived on this when I was dating you?"

Theo gripped me tighter. I was practically pulled onto his lap.

"Yup. I never brought you home with me." He winked.

"I will kill you in your sleep," Theo threatened.

"I'd like to see you try."

I ignored them. I still had so many questions. "You saw the article and came back to Desolate?"

"It was a tabloid, but it was the first news reference to our family in decades outside of the typical, 'This is why we have the peace agreement in place,' bullshit. I wanted to see for myself. So, I hung around Sparkling. When I didn't see anything, I went deeper into the towns surrounding it. That's how I found douchebag extraordinaire, Chuck. I only let him live so I could find you. He ran his mouth off to anyone who would listen about how he knew who Theo was. I had nothing better to do, so I stayed around his building. If I would have known about the boat, I would have warned you."

"Did anyone else from our family survive?" Theo asked, his voice barely loud enough to hear.

Arbor's face dropped. "No. The only reason I'm alive is because I was asleep. The sounds never woke me but the smoke burning my lungs did. I barely got out of there. When I saw what was happening, I ran back in and grabbed my father's wallet. I don't know what made me do it, but instinct drove me toward it. Then I ran as far and fast as I could." He shook his head. "It's a story for another day when I want to bare my soul. Can we go inside instead?"

Theo nodded. "Be careful. Your boat is bigger than we've had."

Arbor was great at navigating the boat. He did it with ease. I was a bit jealous. While I loved driving our boat, I wasn't nearly as confident as he was. Then again, he lived on it for I didn't know how long. He would be familiar with it.

The awe on Arbor's face when he got off the boat was something it seemed everyone felt when they arrived here, except for me. I was confused as hell. We unloaded the boat, putting everything away, then Theo took Arbor on a tour of the castle. They had a lot to talk about, though Theo hadn't exactly warmed back up to his cousin yet. That had something to do with me and the fact that Arbor knew how my lips tasted.

It wasn't much later when Arbor and Theo found Zeke and me in the kitchen getting lunch ready. Zeke still had to pick out a room. I didn't think he'd want to stay in mine. Yes, I was sleeping in Theo's bed every night, but all my things were still in there.

We brought food to the table and sat down to eat.

"Are you staying?" I asked Arbor.

"For now. There's a lot we need to discuss. A lot Theo and I need to catch up on. But first, I need to fill you in on what I found out. Chuck wasn't the one pulling the strings anymore. He blew up the boat, was a massive dick, but he was minor compared to who was behind everything."

"Who is?" Theo asked, his food forgotten.

"The Kades."

"What do they have to do with this?"

"Seems when they heard about the Ostin heir's return, they went and sought Chuck out. Paid him to do what he had to, so you'd be drawn out. Chuck took it to the extreme by blowing your boat up. I figured he would have done something easy since he didn't come off as a guy who was smart. Anyway, I hung around one night, in the shadows of course, and Chuck was out on that rust bucket they called a balcony talking to his equally disgusting friend. He went on and on about how the Kade family reached out to him. Offered him all this money to get Theo out of hiding. It worked."

"But why?" I asked. "What would the Kade family care about Theo being alive?"

"It wasn't widely known, but my father and Roland Kade didn't get along," Theo said. "Did you ever hear the story about the Kade family and how one of them killed their wife?"

"Yes, he murdered her while she was asleep because he wanted to marry the woman he was cheating on her with."

"And his son found out it was his father who murdered his mother and got revenge by killing his father."

"I'd heard that too."

"The son was Roland Kade. The mistress was an Ostin. My grandmother's sister. While no one blamed her since she didn't know what was going to happen, Roland has always hated my family."

"Oh my god. How did I not know that?"

"It never became public information. Both sides of the family kept it as quiet as they could."

"What happened to your grandmother's sister?"

"She felt horrible. Didn't want any of that to happen. Ended her life with a guillotine."

"I'm sorry, Theo."

He gave me a small smile. "It's okay. It was a long time ago."

"And now Roland is taking something that happened before you were born out on you."

"It appears so."

"Holy shit," I whispered. This was crazy. I felt like I was living in some sort of fucked-up movie. How much more was there that the public didn't know about?

Theo reached forward and grabbed a bottle of soda to open it. He didn't drink it often but every once in a while, he liked to have it.

Conversation around me continued. I was too wrapped up in my head though. It felt like there was a giant puzzle that I was trying to put the pieces together on, only none of them fit. But this, what I just learned, it made sense. It was why the Kades were after Theo. Now with Arbor alive too, would he be at risk?

A strangled sound pulled my attention to the people in front of me. Arbor jumped out of his seat to rush over to Theo who had his hands around his own throat.

"Theo!" I pushed my chair back and went to his side.

Arbor pulled him out of the seat and positioned himself behind him like he was about to do the Heimlich maneuver but before he got his arms around him, Theo lunged forward. His eyes were fully black now, with a white ring where his normally dark iris would be. And those different looking eyes were focused on me.

I jumped back, not sure what was happening. Theo got his hands on my arms. His grip was so tight I thought he was going to break the bones.

"Theo, stop!" I cried. "That hurts."

Then his fangs appeared.

28

THEO

What the hell was happening to me? I wasn't in control of my body. It was me moving, me hurting Paxton, but I couldn't stop. Nothing I did would get me to let go. It was like I was a prisoner in my own body.

I heard Paxton's cries. Saw the pain on his face. It was killing me. Ripping my heart from my chest.

Powerful arms around my waist threatened to snap my spine with the force they were pulling me back. It had to be Arbor. No one else would be able to hold me like that.

"Let him go, Theo," Arbor growled in my ear.

I would if I could!

My lips wouldn't work. My tongue was useless. What the hell was happening to me?

Pain shot through my body like I'd never known. My vision blacked and I fell to a crumpled heap on the floor.

"Are you okay?" I heard Arbor ask.

He must have crushed my internal organs. The pain was so intense.

"I'll heal," Paxton replied. "I've been drinking Theo's blood."

"Good or else I was going to offer you mine."

The fuck you will! I screamed in my head. Even through the pain I had enough sense to want Arbor away from Paxton.

My arms were pulled up. A sickening snap followed that had me crying out inside. Arbor was breaking more of my bones. Then I was dragged by those broken limbs. My vision started to come back, fuzzy at first. The ceiling was above me. I was picked up and dropped onto something hard and unforgiving.

"I'm not sure if you can hear me, Theo, but I'm going to tie you down," Arbor said.

My head started thrashing from side to side while my legs kicked out the best they could. It wasn't movements I was making. I still had no control.

One of my fangs nicked my bottom lip causing it to bleed. The taste flooded my senses, causing me to writhe more. A guttural cry came from me.

"Shit, Zeke, go get the rope from my boat. Hurry!"

Arbor appeared above me, his legs straddling my waist as he held my shoulders down. He was clear, the fuzziness gone. "I will break every bone in your body if I have to. You're not getting near Paxton or Zeke."

Paxton edged into my line of sight. I tried lunging for him with a hiss. "Blood," I grated out in a voice I didn't recognize.

"Theo, if you're in there, fight this," Paxton said. Tears fell down his cheeks. He was holding his arms where I held them before. I hurt him. What was I doing? I needed this to stop.

I looked up into Arbor's eyes, wondering if he could see the real me in here. See me pleading.

Kill me, Arbor! I don't want to hurt anyone!

"You're going to get through this," he said. "We'll do it together. I'm not letting you go and I'm sure as fuck not going to kill the only alive family member I have."

My knee came up, nailing him in the thigh. He jolted forward but easily righted himself.

"Nice try. Do it again and I'll crush your kneecap."

Zeke came running back into the room. I could hear his panting.

"Throw it," Arbor said. "I don't want you near him."

The rope landed on what I'd figured out was the dining room table.

"You're going to have to help me, Pax. I need you to loop the rope around the table legs. And bring it up over his arms. Do it fast before his bones fully knit back to together."

I was still thrashing the best I could, nicking my lip repeatedly to get that taste of blood.

"There was something in your drink, Theo," Arbor told me. "It had to have been. You were fine one second and not the next. Someone drugged you. Tampered with your supplies. They must have done it while you were in the apartment building. Sneaky fucking Kades. They really planned this shit out."

Arbor helped Paxton tie my arms down then leaned back and broke both of my femurs. The pain was relentless between things mending and Arbor breaking more. I understood why. He couldn't tie my legs up when I could easily move them.

"You doing okay over there, Zeke? I don't want you passing out on me, man."

"I... I've never seen anyone break a bone. And you do it with ease. I can't watch anymore."

"I'm a vampire. Strength is something I have in spades. And if Theo could talk with any sense of clarity right now, he'd beg me to make sure he doesn't hurt either of you. Why don't you take a seat and keep your eyes closed? I can't catch you if you faint."

Arbor and Paxton secured me to the table. They stood on

either side, looking down at me. I craved blood. Not the real me trapped in this horrific nightmare, but the me who had control.

I felt the moment my arms healed and used all my strength to pull on the ropes. The table was made of wood, something I could easily break. Luckily, Arbor knew exactly what I was doing and jumped in to snap both of my wrists. I screamed in pain, except no sound left my lips.

"I'll keep breaking your bones until this wears off. I'm not sure how long it's going to take so this could be a painful night for you. Paxton, Zeke, why don't you two go to the other side of the castle. I don't think Theo would want you to see him like this and I'll feel better if he can't get to you. Better yet, take my boat out. Come back in a few hours to check in. It's stocked with food that's safe. No one will come near you. It's fully legal."

"I don't want to leave him," Paxton whispered. His eyes were on me. It was pure torture that I couldn't communicate with him.

"Pax, look at me," Arbor told him. "Theo wouldn't want you anywhere near him. Not while you're still human. And not while he has the ability to kill you. If you love him, you'll go. If he actually hurt you, he'd never forgive himself." Arbor didn't know me well enough to understand my thoughts, which made me wonder how much of what he was saying was coming from inside him. I wasn't the only one damaged from that night so long ago. Arbor had to have been too.

Paxton nodded and peered down at me one last time. "I love you. Don't give up. Fight. Come back to me." He choked on a sob and was gone. Out of my sight, maybe out of my life. If I didn't come out of this, I didn't want to live. Arbor would have to sever my head from my body. It wasn't like I had any wooden stakes lying around the castle.

I was dying inside. Completely shredded open at what I could have done to Paxton had Arbor not been here.

The Ostin Heir

"It's not your fault," I heard from my side before Arbor came into view again. I wasn't thrashing like I had before, but I was moving if I could. Both humans were gone. The temptation wasn't here. That didn't mean I gained control back. Far from it. I was still trapped.

"You're going to beat yourself up, Theo. I know because I'd do the same. But there was something in your drink. I was able to save it. Maybe we could take it to a mage to have it looked at. Find out for certain if there was something in it. Then you'll know. You didn't do this because of some fucked-up genes inside us. It was purely induced. Once you come out of this, I'm going to need to head back to the coast and get us more food. I don't want anyone eating anything here. Who knows what else was spiked? I've got enough food on the boat to hold us over."

Arbor kept talking to me. Telling me stories of his travels, keeping things light. I eventually heard the boat come back in. Heard Paxton's voice, but Arbor made them leave again.

As time wore on, he had broken almost every bone in my body. They'd heal and he'd break something else. He punctured my lungs. Cut open my legs. It was gruesome but it kept me in place and in the end, that was all I cared about.

Arbor helped himself to my blood supply since he doubted Novus would let someone convince her to poison it. Novus had a living to make, and she couldn't do that if she wasn't trusted.

Achingly slowly, I was able to form words. Ones that came from me, not the monster. Arbor knew it too. He could hear the change in my voice.

Paxton and Zeke eventually gave up and took the boat out for the night to sleep. It made me relax. If Arbor untied me when he thought I had control again, I didn't want to lose it and go after them.

Hours went by before he was able to stop damaging every part of me.

"Fuck, this is draining," he said. "I can't imagine what it's doing to you."

"I'm tired," I replied.

"We're going to sleep for days once you're out of this and we have safe food in the castle."

"I want you to stay here. For as long as you want." He was here and it felt right. Like this was where he belonged. He was an Ostin after all. Plus, I wanted to know he'd be nearby if something happened to me again. If what Arbor was saying was right, I didn't have to worry. The thought of me hurting Paxton was solidified now though.

"You wouldn't mind?" There was a hint of vulnerability in his voice.

"We just found each other."

He nodded. "I'll stay for now. Besides, Zeke is cute as fuck. That blush of his is adorable."

"Arbor," I groaned. He was a handful when we were kids. Fun, but he would drive his parents crazy. Nothing changed. He was going to be fun still and most likely make me want to strangle him.

But I owed him everything. He saved me. Saved Paxton and Zeke. I could never repay him.

"Think I can untie you now? Your eyes are back to normal."

I did a mental check of my body to make sure there was nothing left of that monster who took over. "I think I'm good but don't go far."

"I won't." He started untying the knots. They were pulled so taut from me yanking on them that he gave up and just broke the ropes with his bare hands.

My body ached all over. Nothing like the pain I had when Arbor was breaking my bones. This was soreness from constantly healing.

Arbor went into the kitchen and came back with a bag of

blood. "Here, this should help. Or you could drink from me." He shrugged.

"I've never drank from a vein before."

"You're missing out. But if you're going to sample me, don't get handsy."

"You're not my type."

He grinned. "No, but Paxton is. So, he's your fiancé, huh?"

"It's new."

"Only you would live your life on an island and have the man of your dreams literally come to you."

"What's that supposed to mean?"

"I was jealous of you when we were kids."

"We were young. What could you have possibly been jealous of?"

Arbor looked down at his hands. "Your parents loved you, always doted on you. Mine were there, sure, but they didn't shower me with affection." I tried thinking back to my aunt and uncle. To how they were with Arbor. I remembered them being kind to me.

"You were always at my house," I said, the memories coming back.

"We were both only children. My parents liked to drop me off there and go do whatever they wanted without me around."

I shook my head. I was young and didn't realize what was happening all those years ago. Dropping down from the table, I went over to Arbor and put my hand on his shoulder. "We're family. I'm not going anywhere."

"Thanks." He smiled up at me. "I think we should get some rest. The guys won't be back until the sun is up, which gives us about five hours."

"I'm nervous to be around him again."

Arbor stood. "What happened to you was a direct result of what was in that soda. Just don't eat or drink anything else that we brought here yesterday. After we've slept, we can start getting rid of what needs to be thrown out. I'll dispose of it when I go back to pick up more food for us or we can burn it."

"When?"

He cocked his head, eyeing me curiously. "Why?"

"To be alone with Paxton, I..." I turned my head, hated feeling like this. Like I couldn't trust myself around the man I loved. The man I'd literally lay down my life for.

"I'll stay until we know you're good. I have food on the boat. I'll even get us more blood from a mage."

"They could recognize you."

He shrugged. "What the hell do I care? I only kept my identity a secret because I was alone and didn't want the weight of the world on my shoulders." He slapped me on the back. "But now you're here to shoulder some of that shit. Let's reclaim our name. Show them we're not who they think we are."

"You're much more confident than me."

"We're Ostins. Besides, we have a royal family to go to war with."

29

PAXTON

Was it possible to wear a path on a stone floor? I didn't think it was because I would have done it by now.

Theo hardly talked to me for two days now. When Arbor gave us the all clear after we returned in the morning, I rushed to Theo, held him as tight as I could. He barely returned the embrace. Instead, he apologized profusely. Shook in my arms with the emotions barreling through him and the guilt he felt. No matter how much I told him it wasn't his fault, he shut me out.

He was locked in his room, only allowing Arbor in to bring him food or blood. Theo didn't trust himself. I understood. This keeping me away was going to stop though.

I went to his room, pounded my fist on the door. "Theo, open up. I'm sick of this. Let me in." I wanted to threaten that I'd leave just to get the door to move, but he'd probably think that was for the best and let me go.

Arbor came up next to me. "You ready? I've been waiting for you to put up a fight."

"Fuck you," I growled but it sounded nothing like when Theo did it.

"I like you much better this way, Pax. Theo brought something out in you. You're not timid and shy like you were when I met you."

"A lot has changed since then."

"You can say that again," he muttered. Arbor reached out and turned the doorknob. It opened. Easily. "It was never locked."

"I hate you so much."

The grin I got in return made me want to punch him. "I'll leave you two be. I'm sure Zeke will keep me entertained."

"Arbor, you have to be careful with him. He hasn't had it easy."

"That's the theme of this castle. Destructive pasts, broken hearts, bleak present, but the future looks bright." He held out his palm and a ball of fire appeared in it. "Feel that heat, Pax. There's a life to reclaim for all of us. And if I have to kill the whole Kade family to do it, I will." He balled his hand, putting the fire out and left without another word.

Looking at the partially open door, I straightened my spine. I was going to do this. Confront Theo. Tell him this shit had to stop. I loved him and I was here to fight for him, for us.

I used my foot to push the door the rest of the way open, slowly revealing Theo sitting on his bed with his back to the door and his gaze on the open windows.

"I knew you'd come eventually," he said, his tone resigned.

"If I waited for you, I'd die of old age." I meant it as a joke. He turned his head to face me, and those eyes broke something inside of me. "Theo…" I went to his side. He stiffened but didn't pull away when I reached for him.

"Paxton, I don't want to hurt you."

I leaned back. "What do you think you've been doing by keeping me away? I want to be with you. When I'm not it's like my heart is trying to break free from my chest to find you. So stop, right now. I'm not walking away. I'm also not going to let you continue to drown in guilt. You didn't hurt me on purpose. It wasn't you."

Arbor hadn't left the island since everything happened. That was changing today. I was over this tiptoeing around Theo shit. They were going to reclaim their name and I was going to reclaim the love of my life.

"I want you to change me. Today."

He reeled back like I struck him. "Why would I do that?"

"Do you really think I don't want to marry you anymore?" I reached up and pressed my palm to his cheek. He hadn't shaved recently. The hair was coarse against my skin. "I love you. We're still getting married. Arbor is going to go get your soda tested. We're going to figure this out. Until then, you're going to change me. Then you won't hurt me. I'll be the same as you." I'd been saving those words for last, knowing they'd hit their mark. They did.

His voice shook. "Are you sure?"

"Yes. I'm not letting you go."

"It's going to hurt."

"I figured it would. I heard after that it gets really good. I've missed being with you. Missed your lips and your tongue. The way you hold me. Touch me."

He groaned, "Paxton."

"You want me, Theo?" I canted my neck, offering myself to him. My heart raced with anticipation and trepidation. I wanted this but that didn't mean I wasn't afraid of the pain I'd feel.

Theo's lips parted, showing off his fangs. His fingers trailed down my neck. "I'll drain half your body of blood. Your heart will slow but before it stops, I'll feed you my blood. I'll push my magic into you. Each family uses their powers to change someone. I've never done it but remember my father telling me how.

It's going to hurt when my magic enters you. I'm darkness and light remember. The fire will burn but I'll be here to ease your pain. When you come to again, you'll be a vampire."

"Will you make love to me then?"

He swallowed. "If that's what you want."

"More than anything."

"Yes."

"We should probably tell Arbor in case something happens."

I took his hand in mine. "Arbor has no place in this. It's between you and me. I trust you." I said those words a lot to Theo. They remained as true then as they do now.

"Sit on my lap. I want to hold you as I do this."

I moved so I was straddling his waist. My head tilted, offering him my neck, my vein.

"I love you, Paxton," he whispered then pierced my skin with his teeth.

The pain was instant from his bite. Sharp, stinging. But with each pull of my blood, it faded, and weakness took over. Exhaustion. Theo was sucking the very life from my body, swallow by swallow. That didn't hurt. It was just draining.

He gripped my hips tightly, pulled me forward. His dick was hard pressed against me. Moans slipped from his lips. He started grinding against me. I didn't think I had enough blood in my body to plump my dick up, but the feel of his desire for me was powerful.

His moans got louder. The sucking stronger. My eyes were barely open. My mind fading.

Theo's teeth left my neck. "Fuck, Pax. I've never felt anything like this," he panted. His wrist pressed to my lips as he tipped my head back. "Drink, My Love. Swallow my blood. Replenish everything you lost."

The first trickle of blood down my throat was warm with

the flavor of cinnamon I craved. I could barely swallow. When more came, I started working my throat. The energy I'd lost was slowly building back. I latched on to him, drinking, sucking.

Theo lifted me in his arms and moved us, so I was lying on the bed and he was over me. He started removing our clothes without my lips ever leaving his wrist. He tore our shirts clean off our bodies. Every second that ticked by my body grew stronger. He had to slice open his wrist repeatedly since it kept healing.

He moved us fully onto the bed and positioned himself over top of me to line our dicks up. I was hard and aching. Power rushed through me making me shake.

Something burned in my mouth which quickly turned to pain. I cried out and pulled back, my gums felt like they were being sliced open. My hand flew to my mouth.

Theo took my wrist in his hand. "You're doing so good, Pax. We're almost done. I need to give you my power now. It's going to hurt."

I couldn't do anything but whimper. I wasn't afraid. I just wanted it over with.

Theo placed his hands on my bare chest. His eyes held mine, his going completely dark. A bright light flared between us. My chest burned like my skin was being charred from the inside out. I screamed as it flowed through me, down my abdomen to my waist, down my legs. It went up my neck to my face, up my arms. Every part of me felt like I was being burned alive. Screams kept tearing from my throat.

I was shaking badly as it started to recede. Something soothing came over me. I drifted in and out. Desolate kept coming to mind and the way I always settled when I was there. Like a blanket to my soul. This calm.

"Come back to me, Pax," I heard from a distance.

Theo.

Fighting against my mind, I tried clawing to the surface. Everything was dark when I blinked my eyes open. It was then I realized I had tears streaming down my face. "Theo," I barely got out. My voice was raw, my throat pained.

"Shhh, you screamed yourself hoarse. It will heal shortly."

Theo held me close, his arms around me, as he pressed kisses to my temple. We were still naked, though I didn't feel his hardness against me anymore. Just the thought of how he was lined up against me before had my body responding. I curled closer, needed more contact with him. The pain was completely gone now.

My dick came to life quickly. I started humping against his hip.

A moan came from him. "Pax, are you okay?"

"Pain's gone." My voice sounded more like my own. I was healing. "I need you, Theo. Please."

He rolled me to my back much like he did before. This time he gripped my thighs and spread my legs. Everything around us was still dark. I couldn't see in front of my face.

Something cold dripped down my crack. I was exposed to Theo, completely open. His finger swirled over my hole before pushing inside. He slowly stretched me until I was begging for his dick. If he didn't get inside me soon, I was going to reach into his nightstand and pull out the dildo I bought. I was getting fucked one way or another.

But he didn't make me wait long. He brought his dick to where I needed him most and started pushing inside. My hands skated up to his chest. Down his stomach. I felt every muscle coiled tight. He was solid. I reached around to grip his hips and pulled him flush against me with minimal effort. We both moaned loudly at the sensation. I guess I had his strength now. Did that mean...

I pictured drinking from him in my mind. From what I

knew, vampires didn't get an insatiable need to drink all the time. They didn't become wild with it except where Theo's family was concerned, but now we knew that wasn't what we thought.

This was me with my fiancé. The man I loved above all others.

Pain pierced my gums, not as intense as it did last time. I lifted my hand and felt the fangs there, long and sharp. Holy fuck.

"Drink from me, My Love," Theo said, his voice barely a whisper.

I rolled us over with ease then moved so he slipped from my body. Searching the bed with my hand, I found the lube and coated my fingers. I breached him quickly with zero finesse. I wanted to be buried inside him when I took my first drink.

The lube was too plentiful, my movements too hurried. Theo was trying to push back on my fingers as I was pumping them in and out. Good enough. I withdrew them and coated my dick with lube. It was right there, waiting to get in that tight channel.

I paused. "I don't know how to do this."

"You've fucked me before, Paxton."

"Not that. Drink from you."

"Don't think. Let your instincts take over. They won't lead you wrong."

I gave myself an internal shake and leaned down. The darkness still encompassed us. Everything I did was by sensing it. Feeling it. My fangs met flesh. I dragged them up until I felt Theo's shoulder. I wanted his neck.

30

THEO

Paxton's teeth were at my throat. His dick was against my ass. His hands roved over my skin. It was too much and not enough at the same time.

This was better than I imagined. I didn't know what would happen when I changed him. I knew how to. What was needed from me. I wasn't prepared for how he would react. How the pain I inflicted on him would affect me. One second, I was hard, barely holding back from breaching him. The next I was soft with tears running down my face, matching his, as pain wracked his body.

Much as I told Paxton to act on instinct, I did the same as I was changing him. I let the fire burn out and brought my shadows to him. I wrapped us in the cool air, hoping it would chill the pain that resided in him. It made me wonder what happened with the other families. How their powers came into play when they changed a human to a vampire. Each family had a different one. Something unique to them. Mine caused Paxton to scream in agony. Thankfully, it didn't last long. Now I was left with a needy new vampire who wanted to fuck and drink. I was more than willing for whatever Paxton threw my way.

He was hesitant at first, fangs grazing my shoulder. The pinch followed next as he pierced my skin. I made sure to flood him with the cinnamon flavor he loved. When I drank from Paxton, not only was it the single best experience of my life, but he was also so fucking delicious. He tasted like sunshine. I didn't think it was possible to encompass that in a flavor, but Paxton somehow managed it. Brought me back to the moment when the sun first touched my skin after so long.

Paxton took a long pull from my neck. His dick breached me in one fast thrust. I called out his name, arched my neck as he kept drinking. My blood would replenish as fast as it left me.

He drank and fucked. Sucked life from me and pushed in hard. It was exquisite. I didn't want it to end. It would soon because I was barely hanging on. My dick was leaking onto my skin. Paxton's stomach rubbed against it with each thrust. He was fucking me like an animal, and holy shit, it was perfect.

His hands came under my ass to lift me up so he could hump into me faster. He hit that spot inside of me that sent my body ablaze in a very different way than I did his minutes ago.

"Paxton!" I shouted as I came. It shot from me with force. Cum pooled on my skin from the endless ropes Paxton was pulling from me.

Fangs left my neck. Lips were there next. Paxton kissed along my skin, up to my jaw then over to my mouth. He took possession of it and pushed his tongue in as he chased his release.

His hips stuttered, faltering, before he stiffened and let go. His body shook from his orgasm as he filled me, hot inside, branding me as his.

I held him through it, telling him how much I loved him until he collapsed on top of me. I welcomed his weight.

"Shit, Theo," he panted, his cheek resting on my shoulder.

"I know."

"I'm really a vampire."

"You are."

"We're getting married. There's no getting rid of me."

I smiled and finally let my shadows fall away, leaving the room bathed with the subtle light of day. I didn't think I'd ever stop cloaking this area in fog. It wouldn't feel right. It was a part of me and something Paxton loved about Desolate when he visited there.

He lifted his head, smile matching mine. "There you are."

"I thought the shadows would help soothe you after the pain."

"They did. More than you know."

"I'm sorry I hurt you. Not just now but before too."

Paxton's hand covered my mouth. "No more apologies. We're done with that."

I nodded. It wouldn't chase the guilt away. Though knowing Paxton was safe and immortal helped.

He moved his hand and pried his body off mine. Cum stuck to both of us. "We need a shower."

"We do."

Standing, he took my hand in his and pulled me up as well. We went to the bathroom and spent a long amount of time cleaning the cum from our skin, trading kisses and hand jobs. Eventually, he shut the water off, and we got dried and dressed. Paxton wanted to check on Zeke. I wasn't worried since he was with Arbor.

We found them in the library. Zeke had a book in hand and was lying on the couch. Arbor was holding a book as well, upside down. His gaze was on Zeke, not the words on the page.

Arbor's head snapped up when he heard us come in. A slow grin spread across his lips. "There you are. By the sounds I heard coming from your room, I'm guessing you're a vampire, Pax, and one of you fucked the other really good."

"Not that it's any of your business what we do in the bedroom, but yes, Paxton is a vampire now," I told him.

Zeke got up and rushed over to take Paxton's hand in his and dragged him to the couch. He started peppering him with questions. Paxton smiled and tried to calm our excited friend down.

Arbor cleared his throat and motioned for the door. We exited the room and started walking along the rounded corridor.

"I have to head back in," he said. "I want to talk to the mage. Have her test the soda. We need more food. You can come with me if you'd like."

I shook my head. As much as I knew I needed to go back to the mainland, I wasn't ready. Not after everything that happened with me trying to hurt Paxton. Once I knew for sure it was in fact something put in my drink and not a biological quality to me, then I'd go. I'd face the media and whatever hell was coming our way. I'd walk among the humans again. "I can't. Not yet."

"I understand."

"Do you want to borrow my disguise?"

He chuckled. "No. I think once I know your drink was poisoned, I'm going to go there and declare to all the world how not one Ostin is alive but two. We have ground to make up. A legacy to reclaim. And a family to destroy."

"You're not going to publicly wage war, are you?"

"No. I'm going to save that for a text to Roland. Let him know we're back and here to stay. Send him a picture of the results. I'm coming for him, whether you're with me or not."

"I'll be by your side. If it was them. We need proof."

"I agree. But that doesn't mean I'm not going to try and lure the rat out. If it is him or someone in his family, they'll take the bait. Run scared. They wouldn't expect to be caught. Without me, they wouldn't have been. They knew one Ostin was alive but not two. And Chuck ran his mouth enough that we have a solid lead."

I stopped walking at the sound of his name. "I need to kill him."

Arbor slapped me on the back. "Leave that to me. Consider it an early wedding gift. You don't want to go back to the coast yet, and I need someone to take my aggression out on."

"It should be me who does it. It was my fiancé he harmed for years."

"I wish I'd known what he was doing back then when I was dating Paxton. I would have ended Chuck then."

A growl rose up my throat. "Can we not discuss how you've had your lips on the man I love."

Arbor laughed. "It was nothing. We didn't have a spark. Nothing like the heat you two put off."

"What about Zeke?"

"He's afraid of me, best I can tell. I'm not sure I'm ready for a chase. There's too much going on with us and the fucking Kades now, so trying to start something with anyone would be a challenge."

We continued walking until we got to the door that led to the center of the island and stepped outside.

"I still can't believe this was here the whole time," Arbor said as he tipped his head back and looked up at the spires.

"Your bracelet would have allowed you to see it if you came close enough."

"For so long, I felt unsettled. Not sure where I belonged. And you've been here. I could have had you back." He ducked his head down. I didn't need to hear the words to understand how he felt. We'd both been alive and never knew the other existed.

"You have a home now, Cousin. Whenever you want it."

He looked longingly at the boat. "I do love that thing but being here has appeal too."

"I need a new boat."

"You do. Want me to handle that while I'm out? I can put the order in."

"Might as well. Then we can pick it up the next time I'm there."

"It's going to be a wild ride. Once the media catches wind that I'm alive too, they'll try to find us."

I grinned. "Try as they might, they'll never be able to see this island. They could follow us, watch the boat disappear, but they'll not be granted access."

"Hooray for mage spells."

"You can say that again."

Arbor glanced around. "Are you going to do something about this fog? It's so dreary."

"I like it," I heard Paxton say from behind us. Turning my head, I saw him step outside with Zeke. Paxton came over and wrapped his arms around me from behind. "Don't get rid of it."

I placed my hand over top of his on my stomach. "I won't. I had a feeling you'd want to keep it."

"We should reclaim Desolate."

I sucked in a breath. "What?"

"The town. It belonged to your family, didn't it? Others lived there. Humans obviously before everything. But the town was in your family's name."

"Holy shit, you're right," Arbor gasped. "It's ours. We own a fucking town."

"Are you going to break into an evil laugh?" Paxton asked.

"I just might."

Zeke cleared his throat. "I thought the government owned it. That's why it was never rebuilt. To serve as a message to other vampires."

"That was before they knew Theo and I were alive. We could build there."

"No," I said. "I can't go back there. Too many memories."

"What if you do something charitable with the land?" Paxton asked. "Like a show of good faith."

"That's an idea," I murmured.

Arbor tapped his finger to his chin. "It's smart. Let us get back in their good graces so they won't see us trying to kill the Kades."

"We need proof."

"We do and I'll get it."

The four of us stood with our bare toes on the sand, talking for a while longer. If someone would have told me I'd be here like this one day, I wouldn't have believed them. I had my cousin back. Someone I thought I lost years ago. I had a friend in Zeke, who'd proven to be loyal to a fault. And I had the man I loved, who I was going to marry. He was a vampire now. One of us. Someone I was going to spend the rest of my exceptionally long life with.

The happiness I felt inside was foreign. Like it wasn't meant for me. But it was there, and I was going to hold on to it for all I was worth just like the man by my side.

EPILOGUE
ARBOR

Two Months Later

My cousin was getting married. To a man I once dated. In no way, shape, or form did I have feelings for Paxton outside of being his friend. Theo still liked to growl at me occasionally. I wouldn't do anything to jeopardize their relationship or mine with either of them.

Paxton floated the idea of them getting married on Desolate Beach, but Theo didn't want everyone's eyes on them. The world knew about us now. The two Ostins who didn't die after all. For a moment, I wondered if anyone else made it out of there alive. If they had, I'd think they'd have come forward and sought us out, but they hadn't. So, it was Theo and me and now Paxton. He would be one of us as soon as their nuptials were complete. Zeke was officiating. He got certified online.

Zeke.

He was sweet and kind and cared so much about the people around him. I was filled in on all Chuck did to Paxton and Zeke. It was truly a pleasure to kill that motherfucker.

I snuck into his apartment a month ago after doing some recon of when he'd be alone. It was easy getting into the building since that shitbox didn't have anyone manning the lobby or a locked back door, for that matter. Getting into Chuck's apartment required one swift tug on the doorknob. It broke off in my gloved hand. No deadbolt. I strolled right in like I owned the place, shut the door behind me, then surprised Chuck in his room while he was slapping his meat to some of the shittiest porn I'd ever seen. I still didn't understand the appeal of those mustaches men wore in the eighties.

He was in the middle of coming when I threw a blade at his chest. It sunk into his flesh, pulling a gasp out of him as a stream of his cum painted the hilt of the knife. That was a scene I wasn't going to forget. Chuck tried to scramble away, gripped the sheets for purchase as blood seeped from where the blade was lodged. Of course, I had more of them. I let two more fly. One into his thigh. Another into his still weeping, pathetic excuse for a dick. That one I took extra joy in. He wouldn't rape anyone again. He wouldn't breathe in another five minutes.

Chuck howled in pain as I walked toward him with my final blade in hand so I could slit his sweat-covered throat. Which I did. Slowly. It was a true work of art.

One of the things I learned about that particular building was that no one actually gave a fuck about anyone else. Even his neighbor, who he thought was his friend. No one came when Chuck screamed. No one gave a shit when he died. They only cared that he was stinking up the apartment with his rotting corpse.

The cops called it a drug crime. That was thanks to the bags of cocaine I left around the room with some powder spilling from them. No fingerprints on anything. Not the knives. Not the drugs. Nor the few strategically placed hundred dollar bills I left on the floor. Had to make it look like it was a stab and run.

I snapped a picture with my phone before I left that night. It was my early wedding present to the happy couple. Theo nodded his head and smiled when he saw it. Clapped me on the shoulder and thanked me. He wanted revenge but he'd get it when we made our next move. Paxton, however, ran to the toilet once he saw the picture and promptly evacuated his stomach. That was okay. He was still new to this life. He'd have to toughen up for where we were headed though. Going up against the Kades wouldn't be easy.

Someone did in fact poison Theo. It was in his soda. Novus confirmed it. I sent the confirmation to Roland via text message. Told him I was coming for him. There was no point in concealing the threat. He wouldn't go to the authorities. It would ruin his family name. His rude ass didn't even reply. That was fine though. I'd be paying him a visit soon enough.

Today, we were celebrating. Enough of the other bullshit.

I watched the sheer joy on Paxton's and Theo's faces. It made my chest ache. Would I ever have that? I wanted it, but I was fucked up in the head. Then again if Theo could find it, maybe I could too. He wasn't exactly stable when Paxton met him. Still wasn't, if I was being honest. I didn't think either of us ever would be. We'd seen too much. Been through hell and back. And still had demons to face.

Zeke said all the right words then told the men to say the vows they'd written. They were both dressed casually in jeans and T-shirts. Theo let some of his fog roll away, so a single beam of sunlight came down onto the center of the island where they stood in the sand. It almost made tears come to my eyes. Almost.

Paxton and Theo held hands as they faced each other.

"Theo," Paxton began. "Before I met you, I was merely existing. Going through each day to wake up and do it again. It was mundane. I was miserable. But then I met a man on a pier who would forever change my life. Leven picked me out of many others. You said he was a seer and I'd like to think he saw this coming. That you and I would fall in love. I wish he was here today to see this. To see how happy you are. Witness you getting married. You hold my heart in the palm of your hand. It's yours to do with as you wish. You're the first person I've ever trusted with anything. I know you'll cherish it just like I will yours. I love you, Theo Ostin, and I'll do so for the rest of my life."

Theo's eyes filled with tears. He didn't let them fall but there was no missing them. "Paxton, you're a gift to me. A man who accepts me for who I am, flaws and all. I have many of them. You take each hurdle we encounter in stride. You stay by me, always there for whatever I need. I can't repay you for what you've given me. You've brought me from the darkness that always seems to surround me and shown me what it was like to feel the light again. Not one I create but one that was there the whole time, waiting for me to emerge. I don't deserve you. Maybe one day I will. Until then, I'll show you just how much you're loved. How much you're valued. I dreamed last night. The first one I've ever had. It was about you and the life we built together. It was amazing. You're my partner, today and always. I love you, Paxton Huxley, until the end of time."

Zeke beamed, said some more things but I didn't hear them. I was too ensnared by that smile of his.

Paxton and Theo leaned in to kiss, blocking Zeke from my sight. They didn't just have a sweet, short kiss. Hands were roving. Tongues met. I thought Theo was going to strip Paxton then and there and fuck him into the water. If he wasn't my cousin, it might have turned me on.

With the ceremony done, we moved inside where Zeke had been working hard all day on dinner and a cake. I learned a lot about him since I'd reunited with Theo. One of those things was that Zeke knew how to cook. I gladly devoured whatever he put in front of me.

Many nights I thought about going back to my boat, drifting out to sea and onto another place. I could easily meet up with Theo when we were ready to storm the Kade castle.

I couldn't leave though. No matter how many times I thought I could, I kept getting drawn back in. By Zeke. Now to figure out what the hell to do with that.

Want a short story from Leven's point of view? You can grab it here: https://BookHip.com/JTVNZDW and sign up for my newsletter.

Next in the series is The Ostin Prince. Arbor Ostin thought he was alone in the world. With Theo back in his life and a new family member, Arbor finally started to feel like life wasn't meaningless. Then there was Zeke. Sweet, nervous, and cute as fuck, like Arbor said. Arbor wanted to get to know him better and maybe it was time to let someone in who could handle seeing the darkness of his soul.

You can also get access to my next book as I write it and much more! Find me on Ream to get all the goodies. https://reamstories.com/michelledare

MICHELLE DARE

NOTE FROM THE AUTHOR

Thank you for reading The Ostin Heir! This is my first solo M/M series. I've written YA M/M in my Paranormals of Avynwood series. If you'd like to check it out, you can find *Craving Camden* on all major retailers. And I've co-written contemporary M/M with my good friend, Rebecca Brooke, under the pen name Haven Hadley. I was nervous going into this new series on my own. But once I got the story idea, I had to write it.

I'm a private person. I don't share a lot of myself online. But in each book I write, I include little pieces of myself. Tidbits I don't normally point out to my readers. I want to with this series.

In The Ostin Heir there are a handful of things. Leven's sticky notes: I have a terrible memory and use them all the time to remind myself of what I have to do. Paxton's migraine: I'm a chronic migraine sufferer who's had them for more than half my life. Theo's anxiety: I have an anxiety disorder and have panic attacks daily. It's often cathartic for me to write about. You'll get more of this in book two with Zeke. The beach: I would live on the oceanfront if I could so I could dig my toes into the sand daily, inhale that salty air, and just breathe.

Note from the Author

Books mean a lot to me both in the stories I write and the ones I read. They allow me to get lost in a world where I don't have a list of medical issues. Where I don't have stress and don't have to think. Where I can *dream*.

I hope you enjoyed this new world of mine. I love the characters and writing their happily ever afters. Most of all, I love sharing them with you.

Arbor and Zeke are up next. I hope you're ready because Arbor never holds back.

Until the next book,
Michelle

BOOKS BY MICHELLE DARE

Series

Isle of Ostin (MM)

Three Ties (MMM)

Ruined & Relinquished (MMM)

Arrow Falls

Salvation

The Heiress

The Vault

Avynwood Pack Origins

Iridescent Realm

Standalones

Daylight Follows

Floating

Christmas on the Rocks

Pleasurable Business

The Unattainable Chief

YA Series

The Ariane Trilogy

Paranormals of Avynwood

Co-Writes

Espen Emperors (MM) with Rebecca Brooke
as Haven Hadley
The Perfect Man (MF) with Michelle MacQueen
as Lynn Dare

ABOUT THE AUTHOR

Michelle Dare is a *USA Today* Bestselling Author. Her stories range from sweet to sinful and from paranormal to contemporary. There aren't enough hours in the day for her to write all the story ideas in her head. When not writing or reading, she's a wife and mom living in eastern Pennsylvania. One day she hopes to be writing from a beach where she will never have to see snow or be cold again.
michelledare.com

Printed in Great Britain
by Amazon